PENGUIN BOOKS

1405

OCTOBER ISLAND

WILLIAM MARCH

October Island

WILLIAM MARCH

PENGUIN BOOKS

Penguin Books Ltd, Harmondsworth, Middlesex
AUSTRALIA: Penguin Books Pty Ltd, 762 Whitehorse Road,
Mitcham, Victoria

—

First published by Gollancz 1952
Published in Penguin Books 1960

—

Copyright © William March, 1952

Made and printed in Great Britain
by C. Nicholls & Company Ltd

To

KLAUS AND DOLLY

Chapter One

AFTER so long a time in residence there, the Reverend Samuel Barnfield and his wife Irma had come to think of October Island as their own, a thing which they themselves had first visualized and then moulded into its plump, gourd-like shape, had coloured theatrically with purples and yellows and greens, and had set down at length in the sapphire waters of the lonely Pacific, but on that first morning, after they had landed from the *Mattie B. Powell*, and stood side by side on the stone mole that ran out into the lagoon, Sam had turned to his wife and said, 'Here is a field that awaits the plough of the Lord.'

Irma nodded absently, but she did not speak, for her eyes, at that instant, were fixed with disbelief on a delegation of natives – a welcoming group who stood with alert and graceful unconcern among a grove of wind-curved palms and watched their visitors with a most flattering absorption.

She had seen immediately that they were naked except for the small fibre aprons of the women, and the rather inadequate breech-clouts the men wore; then, since the truest function of nudity is to make the clothed aware of their own more specialized immodesty, Irma tried the buttons of her shirtwaist to assure herself that they were securely fastened, adjusted her wide, patent-leather belt behind which a watch ticked steadily, and settled her skirts more evenly about her shoetops.

The nakedness of the men, she felt, since there was nothing to impede the muscular, impersonal lines of their bodies, was unremarkable and in no way offensive to her: it was the more focalized nudity of the women that had made her eyes widen in astonishment, for their stuffed, satiny breasts hung arrogantly from shoulder to waist, lifting in rhythm to the breath of their bearers, or vibrating and swaying from side to side as the women yawned or laughed softly among themselves.

Never in all her life – never at any time, nor in any of the strange places of the world, had she seen such a brazen, fleshy opulence, and she lowered her eyes in confusion, thinking, 'We must get clothes on them somehow. That is clearly our first task.'

She turned, as if for confirmation of her intention, in the

direction of the lagoon, her eyes seeking Mr Hansen, the mate of the schooner that had brought them to this unreal and lonely place. He was a young half-breed who inappropriately combined the flaxen hair and grey eyes of his father with the scarcely modified features, the barely diluted skin of his mother's people. She had become attached to him quickly, for reasons she had never entirely understood, and since his English was almost as fluent as her own, they had had long talks together on the slow voyage out.

She located him at once. He was standing alone at the bow of the schooner, and his glance was fixed on the shoreline beyond her. She felt all at once as though she stood in someone's way, that she impeded the view of another, unseen by her at that moment, and she stepped backward in apology, and half-turned her head. She saw then that Mate Hansen's eyes were focused in affection on an old native woman who stood beneath a spreading Hernandia tree, a woman whose eyes, in turn, brimmed over with pride.

'Why, it's his *mother*,' Mrs Barnfield thought. 'He didn't tell me that his mother was still living, or that he expected to see her when we landed. He didn't tell me he *loved* her.'

She bent down self-consciously, as though she had witnessed a thing forbidden her, to pick up a bright, oddly-shaped sea-shell; but she dropped it at once, since it was warm and unfamiliar to her touch. 'But I, too, have breasts,' she thought jealously ... 'Not human breasts of corrupting flesh, but the larger breasts of faith and duty.'

She went forward again, her hand outstretched to meet the familiar hand of her husband, but already he had moved away from her in the direction of the waiting natives. When he was a courteous distance from them, he cleared his throat and said in his thin, vibrating New England voice; 'I am the Reverend Samuel Barnfield, and my companion is my beloved wife Irma. We want to live here with you and share your lives, if that is agreeable to you. We harm nobody. We are peaceful people on a peaceful mission.'

He paused, and Mate Hansen presently stood beside him, translating his words to the inhabitants of October Island. Later, he closed his eyes, raised his face with its fallen cheeks and its imposing, jutting nose to the sunlight, and explained himself, his wife, and their purposes more fully:

They were members of a sect known officially as the Church of the Gospel Prophets, but more commonly called Huhnerites in honour of the Reverend Horace L. Huhner who, in a state of ecstatic trance, had communed deeply with the prophets Isaiah, Jeremiah, and Elijah. Later, under the guidance of these saints, as the imperfect instrument of their holy hands, he had established their faith a generation ago, in the State of Pennsylvania, to be precise.

The Huhnerites were neither a large nor a wealthy church, as were so many others who compromised with the laws of the prophets, he explained; but what they lacked in numbers, they compensated for in piety; what they lacked of wordly possessions, they made up for in energy and loving-kindness ... But no matter how limited the finances of his church were, when compared with others, their Governing Board of Ordained Bishops felt strongly that the ardent missionary was their best ambassador in spreading the truth, and for this reason he and his wife Irma had been sent at length to October Island.

He was well aware, as was his church, that other missionaries of other denominations had visited the island before him, and that all had failed in their hopes, but he did not despair – rather, he took the failures of these others as a challenge, a viewpoint which his wife shared fully. Perhaps the fault did not lie entirely in the sinfulness of the Islanders themselves! Perhaps it lay, somehow, in the lack of devotion and faith of those who had come to show them the evil of their ways!

When he had finished, the natives began to laugh and chatter among themselves, finding the seriousness of this bleak, intense old man both stimulating and amusing; then, recognizing some signal unheard by others, they turned and ran through the trees, towards the beach at the far side of the harbour, and as the women balanced themselves and moved forward, each, in turn, raised her left arm in a ritualistic, supporting gesture, lifting her breasts and holding them outward, as if she displayed a basket of ripe, tropical fruit for others to view and admire.

The men, being unimpeded, ran more easily and with a greater grace, their splayed, prehensile toes curling a little and grasping the sand for support. They outdistanced the women easily, but at intervals, when they saw their companions were falling too far behind, they would pause on the crumbling sand, pivot, and extend their arms to the brown, laughing women.

Sam stood in silence, watching the strange behaviour of the natives. His throat constricted and trembled, as though all the rich words in his heart, the words that his lips could never shape eloquently enough, struggled for release; but Irma pulled at Mate Hansen's arm and said in an astonished voice, 'But where have they gone? Did we offend them in some way?'

Mate Hansen shook his head. He explained that after a proper interval had elapsed, the Radja of the island would appear and officially greet them. Actually the Radja was now concealed behind those flowering shrubs to the left, and had been there since the visitors first landed. He had heard everything that had been said, but since custom forbade one of his position listening first-hand to the prattle of strangers, he must now return to his kampong and wait until his ambassadors had sifted the speech, weighed it, and passed on to him those parts they considered fit for his ears to accept.

'Well!' said Irma in amazement. '*Well*, now!'

After an interval so long that the Reverend Barnfield and his wife had almost given up hope of his appearing at all, the Radja was seen approaching down the beach, followed at the prescribed distance by his three wives. Since the Islanders considered the meeting of strangers not a public occasion, but an affair of the deepest intimacy, he had concealed his casual nakedness under a head-dress of shells and fruit, and the elaborate ceremonial robes of yellow and green feathers that he wore. He paused, in order that all might enjoy his splendour, and stared impassively at the sky; then, flanked by his two advisers, who whispered instructions to him from time to time, he moved majestically towards the four tall lontar palms nearby – the official place of welcome.

His round, dark face had the petulant expression of a cross and pampered baby: his head-dress was heavy, and hard to balance properly; his robes were stifling in all this noonday heat; but no matter how greatly he wished these visitors would stay at home, and not disrupt the routine of his life, the duties of his office were explicit, and they must be fulfilled somehow with fortitude and grace.

All at once, from the grass through which he walked, a host of small, blue butterflies, like crazy, brightly-coloured buttons, rose upward before him, and swarmed loosely above his head in a delirious and shimmering pattern. He waited until their madness had abated, and they had settled once more on the grass, then glancing back at his wives, as if to impress the incident on their memories, he proceeded to the welcoming-place.

When he reached it, he bowed to each palm in turn, for in the sorcerer's world of enchantment in which he lived, there was no difference in the life that abided in a tree, the life of an animal, or the life of a man like himself. He stationed himself in the exact centre of the group, and in a rather flowery speech which bristled with half-concealed meanings, he welcomed the Barnfields to October Island; then, when the traditional amenities had been fulfilled, he added in a more matter-of-fact voice that the visitors who had preceded the ones with whom he was now concerned had not been missionaries but scientists of one sort or another.

They had spent their time spading up the dry beds of old streams, digging in the hills, or searching through the interior jungles; but whatever it was they had looked for, they had not found it, and, in disappointment, they had quit the island some years before, leaving behind them the house they had built for their comfort, many books, and a few pieces of furniture. The house was still intact, and the Reverend Barnfield and his consort were welcome to live there as long as they pleased as the guests of October Island.

Already a group of local housewives were sweeping, mopping, and scouring the place to make it clean and habitable; already workmen were repairing the roof and the walls where time had damaged them. Perhaps, later on in the afternoon, when the young people had recovered from their nervous amusement, they would see that the strangers' belongings were safely transported from the harbour to their new home.

When he had finished his address, the Radja stared appraisingly at Mate Hansen, who had translated his speech into those rapid, barbarous sounds which he could not understand, but which the missionaries had understood readily enough. He felt ashamed, and somewhat put upon, that one of his subjects, a man born on this island that he governed, should possess knowledge denied himself, the ruler. This commonness of speech with outsiders, he thought, this familiarity with their habits and the everyday

11

pattern of their lives, alienated Mate Hansen – to the precise degree of the knowledge that was not shared – from both his ruler, and the ordinary inhabitants of October Island.

He remembered that, in the translation of his words, Mate Hansen – who had even repudiated his musical native name for the coarse name of his foreign father – had occasionally smiled and raised an eyebrow in a significant and most amusing way. Perhaps at such times he had also commented humorously on the text of his ruler's welcome, or had interpolated little explanatory jokes on his, the Radja's, appearance, or on his known foibles. The shape of a face, or the colour of a skin, was easy enough to determine: he, and all others, could estimate by glancing at Mate Hansen what part of his blood belonged to October Island, and what part belonged to the outside world; but who could determine the shape of a mind, or the colour of a thought? ...

This seaman, then – this half-native, half-outsider – whom he was expected to understand, was more baffling to him in reality than the missionaries themselves; for since they were all-alien, all-peculiar, he need make no effort to understand them at all. They, at least, through the very totality of their oddness, had achieved a certain perverse consistency of their own, a certain reversed, but comprehensible clarity in his mind.

With these thoughts to beset him, he straightened his head-dress, and turned back to his duties: the four lontar palms, set so exactly in their square, so equidistant from one another, were all females, and all were now in flower. It was a tree of importance to the Islanders. From its blossoming stalk, both a refreshing drink and a sustaining sugar were made, so that now, as the Radja prepared to return to his kampong, to win the favour of the trees, and to lessen their resentment later on when their stalks were crushed, he again bowed formally to each, and to each he whispered flattering words in turn, for, as everyone knew, one had to be more careful in one's relationships with rocks and trees and animals than one did in one's relationships with men, since there were few ways of learning the wishes, or determining the weaknesses, of these other more subtle and speechless lives: one could never be sure when they were offended, or, if they were, how properly to placate them.

The vexed tree, which before had seemed well-disposed towards you, could fall and kill you as you walked through the forest; the displeased fish, which nourished you with its flesh, could poison you with its anger as well, and send you retching and trembling to the beach; the discontented rock, that had been fixed for ages, sometimes toppled and wiped out a village; the petulant volcano, which had been quiet for generations, could, if its resentment were aroused, explode, and obliterate an island . . .

When his ritual of appeasement was ended, he joined his wives in the grove where they awaited him. At his approach, they went off into peals of unreasoning laughter, patting his cheeks with the palms of their hands, pulling at his earlobes, and poking him with their forefingers until his sullenness had disappeared. He bent down, and they removed his head-dress and his robes; then, running before him, tossing their heads and looking back over their shoulders, they urged him to hurry, as his noonday meal waited him in the village.

Later, when there was quietness once more, Irma turned back to the mole, and the schooner anchored there, and in the pure, shallow water of the lagoon, the fragile hull of the ship was outlined clearly. She could see the thin anchor-chain as it cut at an angle through the water, and the three flattened, brilliantly coloured fish that swam untiringly around it in a fixed and idiotic pattern; she saw the anchor itself as it lay like the abandoned toy of a child atop the yellow sand and the pink, monotonous coral.

The schooner had seemed neither frail nor small while she had been aboard it, and only yesterday she had thought of the anchor and its chain as things capable of holding any object firmly, under any stress or condition; but now, seeing them from this point, in this light, she was suddenly filled with anxiety.

For a moment her life seemed senseless and of no importance to herself or to others; she doubted her mission, and in that terrifying interval she was amazed at herself for having abandoned so many things that others set store by to embark on her life of thankless sacrifice and deprivation.

She turned and looked up, and saw that Mate Hansen stood at her elbow. She said hurriedly, 'I saw you making signals to that woman on the beach. You didn't know it, but I saw you.'

'I saw you watching me.'

'She's your mother, isn't she?'

'Yes.'

'You must tell me about her. You must tell me her name. We must have long talks together when you are gone.'

Mate Hansen looked doubtful, but he said that his mother's name was Toppateeter, and that he was her only child. She was married again, with another husband to look out for. He didn't think that Mrs Barnfield and his mother would have much in common, but she, of course, must do what she thought best.

'Your first duty is to your mother, I know,' said Mrs Barnfield in a voice which was rather plaintive. 'But remember that I'm your mother, too, in a way – not your mother of the flesh, but your mother of the spirit, which is so much stronger than flesh.'

He stared at her with his grave, light eyes, his brow puckered as he digested this new relationship between them. He waited so long to reply that Irma was afraid she had unwittingly offended him, but at last he said with that placating dignity of those who have been affronted too often and too terribly by the world, 'You are my true and dear friend. That is my only wish.'

At that moment, the captain of the schooner came on deck, and Mate Hansen, seeing him there, joined him immediately. They conversed for a time beside the covered hatches, the captain gesticulating excitedly, the mate nodding absently and glancing about him, as though weary of the captain's volubility, and bored with the limitation of his thoughts. They separated after a moment, having reached some unknown agreement satisfactory to both, and Mrs Barnfield, to fill in the minutes, walked up the beach on a little mission of exploration. She stooped down to pick up shells or pieces of strangely shaped driftwood; she knelt on the beach, as rigid and as completely at attention as a bird dog, to stare at the life in the water below her; she made energetic excursions into the brush beyond the beach, there to inspect the bole of a tree or the foliage of a bush; to appraise, to question, to take possession of everything with a quick, emphatic pat of her hand.

Her husband, watching her from the meagre shade of the lontar palms, sat down and took off his hat, a wide affair of weathered leaves and plaited fibre which the natives of these islands could wear with grace but which looked absurd on anyone else. He fanned himself wearily for a time, then, leaning back against the tree, he closed his eyes, wondering from what source his wife achieved her unending and somewhat repulsive energy.

He, himself, was not at all well: while in Java, some years before, he had come down with one of the mysterious native fevers that one came to expect as an occupational hazard. He had never been able to shake it off completely; for at intervals it returned to fill his veins with fire, or turn his flesh to ice. Even now, at this moment of arrival in a new field, when, if he were to impress his parishioners with his earnestness of purpose, he should be at his vigorous best, he felt an old, uneasy aching in his bones which he had known before, but had never been able to define precisely. At that moment it seemed to him that all diseases found sanctuary in him, while Mrs Barnfield was never sick at all, no matter what she did, or how recklessly she exposed herself . . .

He could hear her farther down the beach, shouting to him to witness some discovery she had made, and he got up slowly, as though determined not to give in to illness, to make the best of things at all costs, and went towards her with an assumed vigour that he could no longer feel.

Chapter Two

LATER on, Irma went back to the schooner, and sat in her usual place on deck while the darker of the two dark messboys brought lunch to her on a tin plate. The hatch covers were now off, and the crew, doubling as stevedores, would soon commence discharge of the cargo. When that was accomplished, the schooner would take on fresh water from the clear mountain streams nearby, and the Polynesian captain, whom Irma considered narrow-minded and proud, and did not approve of at all, would start his bargaining with the natives for their spices, sago, copra, or even their occasional pearl.

The Reverend Barnfield said that he had no wish for food. He stood in the strong sunlight, stroking his head in thought, and then went below to write the final paragraphs of his report to the Governing Board of Ordained Bishops, a report which he had commenced conscientiously on the day he and his wife had boarded the schooner in Honolulu. Almost at once Mate Hansen, looking very young and handsome, Mrs Barnfield thought, despite the tattered undershirt and the faded, blue cotton trousers he wore, came up the ladder with his own food. Irma called to him, and he sat beside her, and smiled.

She swallowed, touched her lips daintily with her handkerchief, and said: 'I've been thinking things over, Mr Hansen, and it seems to me I've no right to expect you to take me on *faith!* Actually, you know little about me personally, and nothing at all about my *background* . . . I will no longer take advantage of your trustful nature, so I've come to the conclusion that I must now tell you something of my early life, and let you decide for yourself if you deem it advisable to continue our association, which has certainly been a most pleasant one, as far as *I'm* concerned.'

Mate Hansen looked up from his food and stared thoughtfully at this naïve, romantic, energetic, humourless woman. Where she was concerned, he had long since lost all capacity for being astonished, so he made a noncommittal sound with his lips, nodded vaguely, and smiled.

'I'm forty-two years old,' said Mrs Barnfield, 'so you see, I'm really old enough to be your mother, or nearly so.'

She waited for his denials, but since they did not come, she went on with her story: she had been born in Pennsylvania, not far from the bustling city of Erie. Her father had been a farmer – and a good one, too – who, in middle life had moved to town and opened a grocery store. One reason for the move had been the fact that Papa was subject to a baffling ailment, one which none of the doctors nearby seemed able to treat, or even to diagnose properly.

During these attacks, the veins in poor Papa's neck would stand out like little ropes, and his face would turn a sort of reddish purple. You had to move the ornaments off the mantelpiece when you saw one of these attacks coming on; otherwise, Papa was just as likely as not, in his suffering, to hurl the clock on to the floor, or to smash Mama's little bisque shepherd and shepherdess against the wall. Sometimes, when the attacks were real bad, Papa's hands would tremble, and he'd be so sick at the stomach that he'd gasp and then throw up.

It had been terrible to watch poor Papa in one of these attacks – all red and strange looking. Her mother used to say they were nothing but common temper tantrums, but this merely showed how little her mother had understood Papa's spiritual nature. In her opinion, the attacks had arisen only when the saintliness of Papa's soul came too suddenly in contact with the sinfulness of of the world about him, and recoiled from it in shocked distaste.

Anyway, when she was a girl, these attacks had simply torn her heart out; but her sister Lurline, who was six years older, wasn't at all what you could call a sympathetic type. Lurline had always been a headstrong girl who liked to have her own way, and had never appreciated what was done for her; and it was Lurline who finally bowed Papa's head in shame. Papa had said from the beginning that any child named Lurline would come to a bad end, but Mama had come across the name in a book, and wanted to call her daughter that. She usually gave in to Papa's wishes, but this time she wouldn't and so Lurline was called that.

Papa, who had been a regular saint on earth himself, had worn himself out trying to improve Lurline's nature, but he hadn't succeeded very well. He had never believed in sparing the rod where the welfare of his loved ones was concerned, and to correct Lurline of her evil ways, to bring her into the paths of righteousness, he had, armed with a trunk strap, spent long hours in her

17

service. Oh, it had been pathetic to see Papa, who had never been a real *strong* man, so tired out after one of these sessions that he had to go upstairs and lie down. Sometimes he was so upset that he couldn't eat his supper; but Lurline never showed any gratitude for the things he had done for her own good. She didn't like to say it about her own sister, but Lurline was a depraved girl, and had been so from the first . . .

'But I'm getting way *ahead* of myself,' said Mrs Barnfield cheerfully. 'You'll see later on what a big part Lurline played in my life, but right now, let me finish telling you about Papa, and how he happened to move south. You see, Mr Hansen, Papa didn't improve nearly as much as he'd hoped to in Erie. I guess the winters were just too hard for his constitution. One of the doctors thought he might have a peculiar form of asthma, and suggested that he moved to a warmer climate as quick as he could, and that's what Papa decided to do.

'It was about this time that Papa heard of a fellow-churchman in New Orleans who owned a grocery on Burgundy Street, with a dwelling-house adjoining, who wanted to sell out for reasons of his own. Well, the upshot of the matter was that Papa bought the store, and the house along with it. That was in 1867, right after the Civil War, and I was fourteen years old at the time. Lurline was about twenty, and already a grown young lady.'

Mrs Barnfield ate the last of her food, put down her plate, and went on to say that New Orleans had been a sinful place in those days, and probably still was, if the truth were known; but Papa, being so unworldly, hardly noticed all the evil and corruption about him. His new store attracted a substantial class of people, and all in all they might have settled down happily except for Lurline's conduct, which seemed to get worse and worse.

Lurline was vain, sly, scheming, and pleasure-loving: when she looked back, it almost seemed as though her sister had been planned by nature to fit easily into the loose, ungodly life of New Orleans. A girl of her sort had little trouble in outwitting the loving, supervising eye of an unsuspecting father, and almost from the beginning she did those sneaky things behind poor Papa's back.

Irma had known from the first that Lurline powdered her face, and sometimes even wet a piece of red muslin and rubbed the colour on her cheeks. Perhaps Mama suspected, but Papa in his innocence was unaware of what was going on. Sometimes he'd say, 'Lurline is the picture of health these days. New Orleans may not have improved her moral nature, but it's done wonders for her complexion.'

Mate Hansen laughed mildly, but seeing his narrator's blank, uncomprehending face, he smothered his mirth quickly and turned over with his fork the food that remained on his plate. There was a short silence, and then Mrs Barnfield went on to say that there was no question but that the Huhnerites were strict. Drinking, profanity, gambling, smoking, and those usual sins resulting from lust – being transgressions obvious enough for even the decadent religions to condemn – were forbidden as a matter of course. So was the use of perfume, feathers, ornamental buttons, dotted veiling, and a host of other things that would take too long to enumerate. She, herself, had accepted these prohibitions without question, since Papa assured her they were the instruments through which Satan corrupted man, and won his soul at the end; but Lurline, who believed nothing, laughed at Papa behind his back and mocked the way he smacked his lips.

Lurline had been friendly with strangers, and was always meeting people, and some odd ones, too; but she was evasive when you tried to pin her down, or asked for information about this one or that. Sometimes, when she and her sister were alone in their bedroom with the lights out, she talked a little about the young men she knew, but since Papa was such a strict disciplinarian, she hadn't dared bring any of them home.

At that moment Sam came up from his cabin. He had finished his letters, and had turned them over to the captain, and he started now towards his wife, but seeing her in such earnest conversation with Mr Hansen, he hesitated and said he thought he'd go down to the wharf and supervise the unloading of their cargo, which should take place at any moment now. Irma nodded impatiently, and when he had gone she continued her story:

Lurline had pursued her evil ways for perhaps a year; then she had met a young married couple, not much older than herself, named Frank and Katie Ledger. She had admired Kate enormously, and had modelled herself after her ideal as closely as possible, even trying to talk in that peculiar way New Orleans people affected. At first, she used to slip off to see Katie in the afternoon, when Papa was busy in the store and wasn't likely to miss her; then, the first thing you knew, she was sneaking out of the alley gate at night, after Papa was asleep, and going to a dance or to the theatre with her new friends, dressed up in Katie's clothes, of course, since she had no fancy ones of her own.

'Was she a pretty girl?' asked Mate Hansen suddenly.

'Why, no, she wasn't,' said Mrs Barnfield in surprise. 'I was the one that was always called "the pretty Huffstetter girl".'

She turned the matter over in her mind, and added somewhat cynically that, in the eyes of men, a woman's appearance was of slight importance provided her morals had reached that state of abandonment they set such store by. Anyway, Lurline had been tall and strong-looking, and Papa, with that wonderful sense of humour he had, used to say when they lived on a farm, that if the mule died he could always hitch up Lurline, and make a crop. Lurline had nice skin, pretty teeth, and a well-shaped mouth, but that was about all. Her nose was too long, and it spread out at the tip. There had been just the faintest hint of a cast in her left eye; and then, too, she had always walked like a duck.

'I don't mean to say I was what you'd call a real *beauty*,' said Mrs Barnfield. 'My face is too square, and I'm too tall and wiry, I guess; but even when I was a child, people complimented me on my *hair*. I can remember people saying to Mama, "What a beautiful shade of auburn that child's *hair* is!" Even now, although you might not believe it, my hair reaches way below my waist. The only reason I can squeeze it all into one knot, like I do, is because it's so fine-spun and silky.'

For some time Mrs Barnfield had been aware of a piercing spiciness in the air, and she half-turned and looked quickly towards the beach. She saw, then, that whole families from the hills were now bringing down their baskets of nutmeg, mace, and cloves, and were aligning them precisely beneath the palms, each family standing beside its wares like pedlars awaiting the pleasure of the captain of the *Mattie B. Powell*. She closed her eyes, sniffed the sharp, pervading scent, and, turning cheerfully back to Mate Hansen, she went on with her story:

'Let's see: we were talking about the Ledgers . . . Now that I look back I guess they weren't such wicked people after all, and I don't suppose they were trying to ruin Lurline, either; but in those days I didn't have much experience, and I believed every word Papa told me. So there I was night after night lying awake in the dark after Lurline had slipped out, wondering what my duty was. Then one night Ezekiel spoke out of the fireplace, and said to me, "Why do you tarry so long? Save your sister while there is yet time! Go now and tell your father where she has gone!" After that there was nothing for me to do but get dressed and tell Papa all I knew.'

Her father had really *exploded* that time! He was so angry that his hands trembled, and he could hardly button his clothes; but when he was ready he went to the address she had given him, and rang the bell. He pushed his way in without a word, and there before him were several couples dancing, and several more just laughing and talking together. Lurline was sitting on a sofa at the far side of the room. A young man was beside her, and they both had wine glasses in their hands. Lurline was all dressed up in one of Kate Ledger's fancy dresses, with some sort of feather decoration in her hair, and when she saw Papa standing there so accusingly, she looked as though she'd faint.

Mrs Barnfield looked down and narrowed her eyes.

'I'm not trying to justify Papa's behaviour in *every* respect,' she said, 'but this was the kind of scene that drove him to distraction! Anyway, he recovered himself quickly enough, walked over to Lurline, and slapped her a few times across her mouth. Then he jerked the glass out of her hand and broke it on the floor; and while the ladies present screamed and drew back against the walls, he pulled Lurline to her feet, and shoved her towards the door. He didn't even give her a chance to take off Mrs Ledger's pretty dress, and as far as I know, the dress was never returned to its rightful owner.

'When Papa got to the door, he pushed Lurline through in front of him, and then turned and called Kate Ledger the Great Whore of Babylon. He threatened to have the police on them all if they ever so much as spoke to Lurline again.'

The messboy came up the ladder to collect the luncheon dishes, and when Mrs Barnfield saw his head rising slowly towards them, she uncrossed her ankles, put her feet squarely on the deck, and lowered her sleeves primly about her wrists. Mate Hansen, watching her, wondered how anyone so modest about her physical being could with no hesitancy at all strip her mind of its reticences, and leave it naked and unprotected for strangers to see. When the messboy had gone away, he asked quietly:

'What did your father do when he got your sister home?'

'He beat her with the trunk strap,' said Mrs Barnfield amiably. 'I was standing outside in the patio, and I saw it all. Oh, it made a terrible impression on me, I must say. Mama, who was usually as meek as meek could be, tried to make excuses for Lurline, but Papa ordered her upstairs, and of course Mama went. But she didn't go all the way this time; she stopped on the landing and began to cry and wring her hands.'

The crew of the schooner had gone back to work, and Irma, conscious vaguely of activity about her, saw that they were now unloading the cargo. The spice growers had gathered closer to the schooner to watch, while Sam stood at one side inspecting each box and crate of supplies, counting each bundle of household goods, each carton of religious pamphlets.

'Papa kept hitting Lurline with the strap, trying to make her ask his forgiveness, and promise never to disobey him again,' said Mrs Barnfield; 'but Lurline just shook her head and stood there with that terrible expression on her face. I thought at the time how much she looked like Papa. Papa was talking so loud that the neighbours on both sides could hear what he was saying. He shouted that Lurline had repudiated his teachings, and had disgraced him in the eyes of God.

'All at once a funny thing happened to Lurline: she turned on Papa and shoved him against the wall so hard that you could hear his head bump. Then she took the strap away from him and hit him across the head and shoulders with it.

'"I'll disgrace you!" she screamed suddenly. "I'll show you what disgrace is!"

'It was the first time in his life that anybody had dared talk back to Papa, and it surprised him so, he didn't know what to do. He tried to get away, to go upstairs, but Lurline blocked his path; and at that minute Mama, who was still on the landing, laughed in a piercing voice and said, "Mr Huffstetter has met his match! Mr Huffstetter has met his match at last!"

'I couldn't stand the sight of poor Papa being beaten like a dog, so I rushed in and tried to stop Lurline. She looked at me like she'd never laid eyes on me before; then she threw down the strap and walked out of the house, without even bothering to take her things with her, while Mama kept laughing hysterically and saying over and over like a parrot, "Mr Huffstetter has met his match! Mr Huffstetter has met his match!"

'After Lurline had gone, Papa had one of his real bad attacks, and Mama and I carried him upstairs and put him to bed. When we got him undressed, he turned on his side and groaned, with sweat rolling off his face. I told him not to worry about Lurline, that she was beneath his notice. Papa took my hand in his and said I was the only comfort he had left. He begged me never to be like my sister, but to be a dutiful daughter to him always, and I swore I would. And I have, too, Mr Hansen. I've kept my word to Papa to this day.'

'Is your father still alive?' asked Mate Hansen.

'Why, yes,' said Mrs Barnfield in surprise. 'Papa is still hale and strong, although he passed his eighty-second birthday last February. Mama passed away years ago, though.'

She waited a moment and then went on with her story: how Lurline had lived for the next few weeks was anybody's guess, but people said she'd taken up with a man she'd met on Bourbon Street, and was living with him openly. Quickly she had become a public character, outstanding even in the New Orleans of her day for the variety of her love affairs, her brawls in bar-rooms, and, most of all, for the obscene bitterness of her diligent tongue. She was always being picked up by the police, and when arrested she used her correct name – spelling it out carefully, so that there would be no mistake; when asked where she lived, she gave her father's address on Burgundy Street.

If she had confined her activities to another part of town, conditions might have been tolerable – but that was not Lurline's way: usually she managed to make a scene where Papa or one of his friends could see her; sometimes, when she was drunk enough, she'd come and stand in front of the grocery store, and make a spectacle of herself, while the neighbours leaned out of their windows and talked excitedly.

Once, Papa called the police, and the patrol wagon came and dragged Lurline away, although she locked her legs round a lamp post, waved her arms about, and screamed that she'd only come to beg her father's forgiveness for the wrongs she'd done him. Papa had been so humiliated that time that he couldn't hold his head up for days afterwards; but he had never called the police again, knowing that that was precisely what Lurline wanted him to do.

At that time there had been a scandalous weekly in town called *New Orleans Sporting Life*, a paper which was read not only by the depraved types of the French Quarter, but by most of the highly respected citizens, too. The editor of *Sporting Life* had found in Lurline's activities a source of rich material. Almost every week the paper carried a story about her, and although Mrs Barnfield had mercifully forgotten most of them, two or three remained in her mind to this day.

For instance, there was the paragraph which had read, in substance: 'Miss Lurline Huffstetter, the vivacious daughter of the prominent Gospel Prophet, Mr J. T. Huffstetter, of Burgundy Street, is in the jug again. The usual charges, plus a new one this time: soliciting in a hotel lobby. Where *does* that girl find the energy for all her activities?'

Or: 'Miss Lurline Huffstetter, débutante daughter of the Burgundy Street grocer and churchman of the same name, is now receiving her friends (and we're told on reliable authority that this gay girl hasn't an *enemy* in the world) at Edna Judge's brothel on Basin Street.'

'Things got so bad,' said Mrs Barnfield, 'that people from uptown, perfect strangers, would come in the store just to see what Papa looked like. It would have been a bad experience for any man, but for Papa, with his sensitive nature, it was awful.'

She waited a moment, to let the thought sink in, and then said: 'Once when Lurline was drunk and walking up and down outside the store, while Papa did his best to ignore her, to pretend that she didn't really exist, I went up and tried to argue with her.

'"Don't you realize that nobody wants you here," I said. "Why don't you go somewhere else?"

'"You *sneak*," she said. "I hate you almost as much as I hate him."

'"What you think of me is not important, I assure you," I said. "It's Papa I'm thinking about. Can't you see that you're slowly killing Papa?"

'"If I do kill him," said Lurline in a loud voice that carried all the way down the block, "let me know in time so I can send him a wreath of poison ivy."'

She had become so interested in her past that she had not

24

noticed how time slipped by; but, glancing up for an instant, she saw that her effects were now out of the schooner's hold, and piled handily on the wharf. As she watched, a group of natives came up, some with thick bamboo poles, others with ropes and slings. They secured the goods, while Sam pointed, cautioned, and gave instructions which they did not understand; then, when everything was ready, they lifted their burdens to their shoulders and started out in a long procession up the beach.

Sam caught his wife's eye, and beckoned with his hand, but she shook her head and turning back to Mate Hansen she said quickly: 'To make a long story short, things got so bad that Papa decided to sell out and go back to Pennsylvania; so I guess Lurline won in the long run, although he always denied she had anything to do with his leaving New Orleans.'

Sam was beckoning more violently, and Mrs Barnfield called out impatiently, 'In a minute! In a minute!'

She got up and walked towards the small companion-way, while Mate Hansen followed her. Over her shoulder she continued: 'In the years that followed, I kept wondering how I could make things up to Papa for the way he'd been treated. I wanted to prove to him that he had one daughter who appreciated all the things he had done to see that she stayed in the path of righteousness; so when a man like Mr Barnfield, who was pastor of a Huhnerite congregation not far from Erie, and who had Papa's full approval, asked me to marry him, I said I would. I did it to please Papa, not myself. I was nineteen years old at the time, and he was fifteen years older. It was to be a marriage of the spirit only. That's the way we both wanted it, and that's the way it's always been. Mr Barnfield's people come from Vermont. They are respectable and highly thought of by others.'

They came down the companion-way together, as Mrs Barnfield went on: 'I didn't have the least idea of being a missionary when I married; but Mr Barnfield heard the call to work in a foreign field, and I went with him, being his wife. We've lived all over the world since that time: Africa, Java, the Philippines, Hawaii, and many other places. This is the first time we've been sent to a place as far away from everything as October Island is. I suppose it's a come-down, in a way.'

She joined her husband on the mole, her mind still busy with her past.

One of the natives came up and spoke to Mate Hansen, and Hansen, in turn, told the Barnfields that the women and the workmen had finished their tasks, and the house was now ready for their pleasure. The last of the porters were disappearing down the beach, around a small peninsula of palms, and he suggested that they follow the path of the porters. The house, he said, could not be missed. It was set on high ground, and it was plain for all to see.

But Mrs Barnfield had not quite finished her story, and as her husband moved off alone, she joined Mate Hansen where he stood inspecting the wares of the spice growers, and said: 'On that last day in New Orleans, Lurline came and stood outside on the pavements to watch the movers crating and taking out our furniture. She was completely sober that day, and she didn't try to make trouble for anybody, but when she caught sight of Papa moving about in the parlour, she said, "Don't talk to me about disgrace! I can show you what *disgrace* really is!" ... Now, you know what I think, Mr Hansen? I think Lurline loved Papa, in her way, and wanted his love and affection in return; but since her disposition was what it was, of course Papa could never give those things to her. I may be wrong, but that's the way it seems to me, now that I'm not nearly so mean and narrow-minded as I used to be.'

The Reverend Barnfield stopped when he reached the grove of palms, and looked back over his shoulder. His wife was still engaged in animated, long-winded conversation with Mr Hansen, and he sat down in the shade to await her. Before him, a coconut which had washed ashore from some other island was sprouting in the crevice of two stones where there was no sand to sustain it, as though determined, somehow, to fulfil the urge of life within itself, even in this inhospitable place of no soil, even on this island where coconuts abounded, and others were unwanted.

He sighed and loosened his collar. He wished that the Governing Board of Bishops had seen fit this time to station him in some austere place of deprivation and want. He had asked to be sent to North China, to Afghanistan, to Alaska – to any land of hunger and silence, where existence was bleak and hazardous, an uncertain struggle that occupied the whole of a man's mind, and left him no time to contemplate sin; but the Governing Board had felt his usefulness lay in other directions, and here he was again, on another Pacific island!

He was sick of these hot and easy places, these corroding lands where everything was a seduction of the senses, a trickery of the flesh. Here, even the fruits and flowers, those innocent things, were designed to divert and entice the unwary – the phallic fruit, the yonic orchid – for they felt and smelled, not as vegetation should feel and smell, but as warm, excited flesh

There were, in these places, flowers that closed their petals or drew back with human coquettishness as you stretched your hand forward to touch them; there were plants that bled as you stripped their leaves; there were vines that caressed the lonely who passed through the forest, seducing his flesh with a touch as delicate as the touch of a woman, and winding about his throat and waist in an embrace so passionate that unless he moved at once, he never moved again; there were those plants with narcotic juices and sweet smells that lay in wait, as though themselves sentient and aware of the evil of their intentions to trap the insect with their lures, to destroy him, to digest his juices with their juices.

He heard his wife calling to him, and he turned once more in the direction of the harbour. She had finished her talk, and now she was coming towards him down the path, striding along with all that distasteful energy. He sighed, got up, and stood there waiting until she reached his side.

She began talking at once about October Island and its inhabitants, speculating, wondering, appraising the possibilities of their success in such a place, but he heard little she said, for his mind was still fixed in other directions, was concerned, still, with heat and fertility and growth. He did not want to question either the method or wisdom of his Creator, but it seemed to him that life should be repeated from generation to generation not through a hot union of excited flesh, but as an impersonal thought in the cool mind of God.

Chapter Three

THE house was situated on a low, green plateau some distance inland, but close enough to the sea, when, at dusk, the shrill chattering of the island was stilled a little, to hear plainly the repeated noise of the surf as it raced forward, lifted, and broke over the reefs with the hissing sound of water spilled on hot stones.

The house itself was the traditional cottage of the October Islanders, but a little roomier, a little taller, a little more imposing than the dwellings the Islanders ordinarily built for themselves. It was set well above ground, on thick bamboo stilts, with an extending overhang so wide that it served the purposes of a porch, and with steps rising on either side of the entrance door to a tiny veranda of laced rattan and palm slats. The walls were of resilient, precisely woven bamboo. For the admittance of air and sunlight, large areas in the walls had been left open, but these elementary windows could be closed with sliding panels of palm fibres. The floors were of polished palm slabs, and the V-shaped roof, with its high ridgepole and bamboo beams, was covered deeply with thatch from the nipa palm.

Later, when their belongings were unpacked and set in their tentative places, Sam said, 'We should be happy here, Mrs Barnfield. We should accomplish something for the glory of the Lord in this place.' Then, not waiting for her answer, he went outside and looked about him.

The plateau commanded a perfect view of Min-Rahabaat, the great, twin-coned volcano for which October Island was celebrated, and during the nine years he was destined to live there, he would often stand outside, as he was doing this first afternoon, and stare upward at the twin cones with a sort of rapt disapprobation.

The volcano was the first thing you saw as you approached the island, and on that memorable day when it had appeared so mysteriously in the distance, seemingly without support above the curving horizon of the sea, he had caught his breath audibly, and moved back from the rail of the ship, awed by the promise implicit in its towering, austere magnificence.

His wife, hearing the sound he made, seeing the expression on his face, came up and said patiently, as though reassuring a child, 'It's nothing but a volcano, Mr Barnfield. It's nothing but a volcano with two cones. There's nothing to be afraid of.'

He sighed, shook his head, and closed his eyes. He was not frightened in any usual sense of the word, but he knew the uselessness of explaining his thoughts to his wife: his emotion at that instant was deeper than physical fear could be, for he was thinking of the power that had made the volcano, and of the greater power that lay beyond that creation, and of the final power so illimitable, so overwhelming that it could not be encompassed in the nervous, finite mind of men.

Then, passing one hand over his bald head, he moved slowly along the deck. Mate Hansen, who was never too far away – although what he and Mrs Barnfield found to talk about so volubly he could never understand – came up at that moment and said that Min-Rahabaat had not been active for hundreds of years; that for purposes of reality it could be considered extinct. It was true, on occasion, that senile, echoing rumbles could be heard from its depths, and at such times streamers of smoke and ineffectual jets of steam issued from its craters, but that was about all. In fact, the Reverend Barnfield and his wife need not concern themselves further with the volcano, for they would be as safe in its shadow as they were on the deck of this fragile, straining ship.

Now, remembering Mate Hansen's words, Sam Barnfield clasped his hands together and whispered, 'I am God's creature. I exist only in His love. What God has willed for me, I shall accept.'

Irma came to the door, her head tied up in a dust-cloth. She had meant to ask her husband to help her arrange their dishes in the outdoor kitchen, but seeing him in an attitude of devotion, she remained silent, and went back to her tasks. She found a certain just appropriateness in her laborious, unimaginative toil of washing, cooking, sewing, and digging in the earth. She left the spiritual side of their mission to her husband, feeling that while he was a preacher whose fervour could move others to repentance and repudiation of their sinful lives, her own usefulness was that of ministering to the dull, everyday wants of the congregation.

In her heart, she knew herself to be a woman of little sense, and of only the slightest moral worth – a restless, aggressive old charwoman of the Lord whose duties were the menial ones of keeping the temple sweet and unprofaned, of seeing that the long, tedious road to salvation was swept and unimpeded.

As she thought thus of the humble purposes of her life, she remembered that her husband had not eaten lunch. She called to him this time, but he said he was not hungry, that it did not matter to him at what hour supper was served. When she had gone, Sam went to the small summer-house that faced the sea and stared thoughtfully at the water he had just crossed . . .

At first, October Island had been only grey cones against pastoral pink clouds, and the soft mauve sky of daybreak; but as the morning advanced, as the schooner came closer, a more detailed composition appeared, and there was then not only volcano, clouds, and sky, but dense vegetation too – a green, undefined mass which, from this distance, resembled loosely knit, ravelling wool; then this grouping of multi-shaded green resolved itself in turn into a wide composition of mountains, ravines, denuded rocks, and flat plateaux – a tableau underscored and separated from the blue of the Pacific by a beach of sand like a white, undulating ribbon.

At one point in the approach to the island, the separate parts of the tableau arranged themselves to form two heroic figures asleep beneath the volcano. The first of these figures was male. He lay with his head towards the east, his muscular throat lifted and arching a little, his face turned towards the sea. One of his legs lay heavily against the earth, the other flexed and upraised. His long arms rested beside his body, the palms turned languidly upward in a gesture of unbelievable grace.

The second of the figures was female. She slept on a level below her companion, and was less imposing in size, less distinct in the clarity of her outline. Her head stretched westward, a little lower than her breasts which lifted so serenely to the sky. One hand was cradled beneath her head, the other was upraised, as if she sought eternally the welcoming hand of her consort.

The Reverend Barnfield, seeing this small miracle of nature for the first time, pressed closer to the rail of the schooner, his curved, harsh nose raised upward, his eyes closed in devotion; for he thought at that moment how, for thousands of years before he had been born, countless thousands of other men, men who had once lived and suffered and aspired, as he did at this precise instant in time, had seen the same mirage from their cata-marans, their *praus*, and their outrigger-canoes, their laughter hushed suddenly at the sight, their hearts filling up slowly with the love and wonder of God.

He went to his cabin for a time, and when he came back on deck, the gigantic figures had dissipated and resolved themselves into the hills, and valleys, and denuded rocks from which the strange illusion had been created. Later, at dinner, he spoke of what he had seen, and the perspiring Polynesian captain, who had recently been christianized, and now despised the abysses of corruption in which he had formerly lived with all the fervour of the true convert, said that he had often seen the mirage, but now no longer found interest in it.

The natives of October Island, he added, knew quite well who the figures were, and their purpose in thus stretching themselves across the landscape: they were the ancient god Rahabaat, and his consort, the top-heavy Kallapaaga, who often came thus on fine days to sleep, sun themselves, or stare outward at the sea. He turned to Mate Hansen for confirmation, and the mate smiled and said it was true ...

And now, remembering the marvel he had seen from the deck of the *Mattie B. Powell*, Sam Barnfield wondered what part of the mirage the plateau where he now lived had been: perhaps a brow, perhaps an open, enormous eye, perhaps an outstretched palm. The thought humbled his pride, and he turned his head and looked to the south end of the island, where the eroded cliffs were, where the grey, avaricious gulls screamed, glided, and darted swiftly for food.

Inside her new home, Irma Barnfield rearranged the small desk on which her husband wrote his sermons, moving it this time to the dining-room, where she considered the light better. She wiped the desk with a soft cloth, but before she had finished her task, she put aside her rag and sat down absently. From where she was, by craning her neck a little, she could see her husband's gaunt profile in the summer-house. She would have liked more than anything to talk to him, to tell him the uncer-tainties that were in her mind, but she did not, for there was no relationship between them but the relationship of missionary and housekeeper, and that was all their union had been from the beginning.

She admired her husband for the qualities of his mind, his pitiless dedication to the good of others, his humility where his own faults were concerned, and, in some ways, for his meek impracticability. She pitied him because she knew, and had always known, that he was really an old writer who could never write a line that was acceptable to himself. He was not at all like her father, either in outlook or temperament, but she could no more have told him her secret thoughts now, than she could have told them to her father as a child.

She sighed and drew an imaginary figure on the desk with her forefinger: her talk with Mate Hansen that morning had made a greater impression on her mind than she had realized, and she thought once more of Lurline, wondering, from this distance in time and place, what her sister's life would have been if Papa had been less harsh in his evaluations, less inflexible in discipline. Perhaps the fault was not entirely Lurline's, after all. Perhaps Papa, despite his wonderful saintliness, had been too unyielding, too unable, from his godlike pinnacle of perfection, to understand the limitations of lesser beings.

She raised her throat and stared in concentration at the wall before her, then shaking her head from side to side, as if in denial of some inescapable fact, she buried her face in her palms, for at that moment she remembered once more the part which she herself had played in her sister's life; in particular, the betrayal that had brought on that final, disastrous rupture. She remembered, too, the expression of distaste on Mr Hansen's face, and how he had first stared at the deck, and then turned his head away so that she could not see the look of condemnation in his eyes as she casually told him how she had revealed to Papa where Lurline was that night.

She shook her head despairingly and sighed, for even after all these years, she did not see how she could have acted otherwise; then, speaking aloud to herself in an apologetic, defensive voice, she said, 'But it was my *duty* to tell Papa! I had no choice in the matter, after Ezekiel spoke to me!'

Nevertheless, the memory of Mate Hansen's disapprobation haunted her, and she sat for a time turning these old matters over in her mind. Then, all at once, she knew that she had not heard the voice of Ezekiel, or the voice of anyone else, from the fireplace. She had deluded herself from the beginning, although one part of her mind had always known the truth: she had heard nothing that night except the verbalization of her own wish, the fulfilment of her dislike of Lurline ... But she was not entirely to blame, she thought defensively, for the hearing of divine voices by maidens had been one of the conventions of her day – an advertisement of innocence, an affirmation of virginity.

Instantly, she saw where her present duty lay, and she got up in astonishment, surprised that the idea had not come to her at once: she would write to Lurline and ask her pardon for the wrongs she had done her in the past, whether consciously or unconsciously, and she would invite her, if Lurline was now poor and sick, with nobody else to turn to for help, to come to October Island and make her home in future with Mr Barnfield and herself. As soon as the idea had taken possession of her mind, she put it into execution, and when the letter was written to her satisfaction, was sealed, with the words 'Miss Lurline Huffstetter' written on the envelope, she sat nibbling at the point of her pen, wondering where to address it.

She had not heard of her sister in almost a quarter of a century, and she had no idea where she was now living. The last information she had had, Lurline had been in Edna Judge's establishment, but surely, at her age, she was not still there. Using her fingers as keys, tapping off the years against the top of the desk in an erratic Morse code of her own, she calculated swiftly: Lurline must be an old woman now, with, perhaps, grey hair and wrinkles, and a fat, bloated stomach.

She got up and walked about the room, saying impatiently, 'Oh, dear! Oh, dear! I wonder where Lurline is *now*?'

And then a most sensible solution of her dilemma occurred to her: if Lurline was still in New Orleans – as she probably was, since she had such a natural affinity for that wicked place – the police would assuredly be in contact with her, her temperament being what it was. The thing to do, then, was to write another letter, a covering letter of explanation to the Chief of Police, and place this second letter, along with her letter to Lurline, in one of the big, official envelopes that Mr Barnfield used for his reports to the Governing Board of Bishops.

She sat down again, took up her pen, and wrote rapidly. She would esteem it a great favour, she said, if the Chief would see that the enclosed letter, whose purpose she was careful to explain, so that he would not think that she, too, was a woman of loose morals, was properly addressed and forwarded. To fill out a page, she thriftily included a description of October Island, and stated what she and her husband expected to accomplish there; then, when everything was finished, she went to the *Mattie B. Powell* and turned the letter over to Mate Hansen, asking him to mail it personally in Honolulu. When she returned, she saw that her husband had moved from the summer-house to the rear of the plateau, and was examining a young palm tree which grew there.

The smooth bole of the tree was of that smoky shade of green seen in some fine jades; and circling the bole, at evenly spaced intervals, were rings of greyish-green; the leaves themselves were a brighter green than the trunk, with yellow spines set at their edges.

He had always loved palm trees, and he wished now that he knew more about them. There were so many kinds of palms, and there were as many lessons to be learned from them as there were varieties. Surely the palm was God's thoughtful gift to those who live near deserts, or in the depths of jungles, or on the hot, lonely islands of the seas. They supplied man with sago, fruits, sugar, syrup, vinegar, milk, and tender green buds for the cooking pot; they gave him mats, clothing, furniture, hats, sandals, baskets, thatch, lumber, and every other useful thing that can be braided, twisted, plaited, or woven.

He raised his arm and touched the lustrous stem of the palm before him in the way that another man would have stroked a dearly loved animal. He did not know the name of this particular palm, nor what practical uses it had for man, but even if it had none at all, its grace alone justified it. Perhaps the purpose of this palm was to lift up man's heart in praise of his Creator.

Mrs Barnfield watched her husband for a time, and then, going swiftly to her outdoor kitchen, she started a fire in the oven in preparation of supper. Sam, hearing the clatter she made with her pots, half-turned, listened, and then went on with his reverie: perhaps man, too, was like the palm tree, each with his special usefulness, each with his unique contribution to make to the welfare of others. He wondered if he could work these vague thoughts into a sermon for the instruction of the people of

October Island. But perhaps the comparison of man and palm tree was beyond their understanding. Perhaps –

At that moment Irma called him, asking that he bring more wood for the stove, and he walked away slowly to do what she asked.

Later, when the meal was prepared, he and his wife ate it in silence; and not long afterwards, having been awake since long before daybreak, they went to bed, and fell asleep at once.

That night they were awakened by music in the underbrush that grew thickly on the mountain side of the plateau. They went outside and stood together in the moonlight, listening. There were bamboo flutes pitched in different keys, there were finger-drums, and larger drums that were tapped at with sticks. There were gourds filled with sand, gourds filled with pebbles, and gourds filled with stones. There was a muted, primitive marimba, and, listening closely, you could hear, when the other instruments were silent, the thin sound of a native guitar.

When the serenade was over, Irma nudged her husband, and he made an earnest speech of thanks; but after he had spoken for a few minutes, he became conscious of the fact that the serenaders had gone, and that he was addressing only the air and the softly tossing palm trees, and passing his hand roughly over his head he sighed and went back into his house.

Mrs Barnfield interpreted the serenade as a most favourable sign, an indication that already the natives of October Island accepted them, and paid them a most courteous compliment of friendship. She wondered if she should have invited the serenaders into her house, but even if she had done so, how could she possibly have entertained them, with half her dishes as yet unpacked?

But she need not have concerned herself with these issues of etiquette, for the concert had been only an impersonal, first-night compliment paid by tradition to all important visitors to the island.

The Radja had ordered the serenade as soon as the Barnfields had landed that morning. He was well adjusted to the oddities of missionaries, and he was determined that his newest, and probably most tiresome, visitors receive all the courtesies due to them by custom, since the snubbed missionary, who had been so earnest in his friendship, so outspoken in his affection for his fellow-man, could, if his zealous anger were aroused, summon a gunboat and shell an island, sending the people there bleeding and screaming to the hills.

Chapter Four

MATE HANSEN took the letter, promised Mrs Barnfield that he would faithfully mail it in Honolulu, and put it away in his locker, where it would be safe. After she had gone, he washed himself with galley soap and water, and with suds clinging to his body like patches of snow he dived over the stern of the schooner, and swam in the blue, translucent water of the lagoon.

He had an unreasoning sense of joy as he up-ended himself, went to the bottom, clutched at coloured shells that he found there, and lifted again to the surface, shaking his straight flaxen hair out of his eyes. It was only in this lagoon which he had known all his life, on this small island where he had been born, at this time of day near sunset, that the uneasiness, the sense of belonging to no certain people, and to no fixed place, as others did, disappeared and left him free for a time to exist in contentment.

When he was tired, he turned on his back and floated; but he saw that the sun was now above the cones of Min-Rahabaat, and he knew it was time for him to see his mother, that he must hurry a little if he were not to keep her waiting. He came quickly up the ship's ladder, and, going to his cabin, he perfumed himself, brushed back his hair, and put on the fresh white suit he had saved for this occasion.

His mother was waiting under the Hernandia tree, just as he knew she would be. She came up to him quickly, and pressed her cheek against his own; then, to observe him better, she leaned backwards from her hips, laughing, fluttering her eyelids, and moving her shoulders about in little coquettish gestures of affection; and at last, tugging impatiently at his hand, she drew him forward, as though he were still a weight she would willingly carry unaided, and they moved off together through the palms, in the direction of her cottage.

His father was Professor Hans Axel Hansen, the famous anthropologist who had once lived on October Island to investigate the customs of its people, and who, plainly enough, had done so with some success. He had left the island when his son, who was also called Axel, was four years old, and naturally the boy did not remember him very well. Now, his most vivid memory of his father was the Professor's almost albino blondness, and the fact that he had worn eye-glasses fastened to one of his pink ears with a thin, black cord.

There was another memory associated with his father's eyes, one which he had never been able to place precisely in either time or setting; but, in the fantastic picture his mind still retained, his parents had been sitting together on a beach when he had looked up from his play and had seen that his father's eyes were ablaze, were shining with a menacing, godlike fire. Now, after all these years, he knew the fire had been caused by a trick of perspective and setting sun, and had no meaning beyond its simple implications; but he had not known these things then, and he had cried out and had gone to his mother for protection. But his mother, who usually laughed tolerantly at his fears, who ordinarily took him in her arms, and sang an Island song to him, this time through chance, or from some deep, intuitive knowledge within herself, had reached out her arm and removed her husband's glasses at once . . . And there again were his father's eyes, pale, preoccupied, and a little watery.

It was the one picture of closeness that he had with his father, and the memory often came to him at this hour near sunset . . .

Outside her house, beneath an old canarium tree, Toppateeter had set the low table on which they were to dine. She had placed coloured mats, which she had woven herself, on the sandy ground, and as her son studied the effect of what she had done for his pleasure, he bent down and put his arm about her waist. At once, she laughed softly and suggested that he take off his beautiful white suit, since she had now seen and properly admired it; and when he had done so she brought him a woven apron with silver tassels to wear – the customary male attire for occasions such as this – an apron not unlike the longer one she wore herself.

She had been aware from the first of the paper-wrapped parcel he carried under his arm, and wondered what gift her wonderful son had brought her, but she was determined this time not to mention it until he, himself, made a formal presentation after their supper had been eaten; but now, as she folded his clothes and put them away, she could contain herself no longer. She picked up the package, smelled it, shook it gently, and then held it to her ear, stamping her foot with simulated petulance.

'What is it?' she asked eagerly. 'What is it, my lovely one?'

But he took the package from her, slapped her affectionately on her fat brown back, and put it away on the rafters below the thatched roof, a place that she could not reach. His mother continued to beg, to implore him to relieve her unbearable curiosity, but he would not. It was the sort of teasing game that his mother loved, and he wanted her to be happy, if he could make her so; for he had long known that she could express her affection for him only in her fluttering gestures, her squeals of pleasure, her coquettish pouts of impatience; but when the game was played out she pretended indifference, as she always did. This time she said, 'But perhaps the present isn't for me. Perhaps it's for that missionary woman who follows you about with her pig eyes.'

'It's for you. I bought it in Singapore.'

He got the package from the rafters, and placed it in her hands. She opened it with cries of wonderment. It was a carved music box with a mother-of-pearl lid. He explained its use, and showed her how to wind it, and when she had done so, she put it on the table before them and opened the lid. At once the strains of a Viennese waltz came to her ears – tinkling, unreal, and remote from any world she had ever known. She clasped her hands in delight, shaking her long hair from side to side; but when she could stand her pleasure no longer, she lowered the lid again, sprang up from her mats, and hurried inside her cottage. A moment later she brought out a pitcher of palm wine, and pickled octopus rings on a wooden tray.

'This missionary woman,' she said. 'Is she in love with you, like all the other girls?'

'Oh, no, no! She's only trying to convert me. She wants me to become a Gospel Prophet.'

'She's a little too old, but not at all ugly. Is she your sweetheart, my handsome one?'

Her son made a sudden gesture of distaste and said, '*Ba-oola! Ba-oola! Fone nar marsanda ramesal!*'

He had heard the expression in a waterfront saloon in Brooklyn, and his translation – 'Please! Please! Not while food is set before me!' – was the best he could do. He had thought the expression witty, and this was the first occasion he had had to use it; but he had not been prepared for the dramatic effect it had on his mother: she fell back suddenly against her mats, her breasts vibrating with mirth and rolling from side to side, her necklaces and anklets rattling and clinking together. Then, turning on her back, her arms upraised as if imploring mercy, she went into peals of wild, hysterical laughter.

'Oh, my son!' she screamed. 'Oh, my lovely, wide-shouldered son! ... Where can you find another as extraordinary as my *son*! So fascinating to the girls! ... Oh, my beautiful, talented one! So handsome, and so witty, too!'

She wiped her eyes on the hem of her apron, and after her mirth had abated, as they drank their palm wine and nibbled at the octopus tips, Mate Hansen repeated to his mother the things he had learned about the Barnfields and their life together; but when he told her Mrs Barnfield had confessed to him that very morning that, although married for many years, she was still a virgin, his mother was first silent, trying to comprehend this, the oddest bit of all the information she had stored up concerning missionaries and their incomprehensible habits; then, when its full significance penetrated her mind, she went off again into paroxysms of mirth, louder even than before.

'No, no!' she implored in delight, her voice echoing through the palm grove. 'Oh, no, no, my darling but simple-minded son!' She tried to sip her wine, but half of it went down the wrong way, and the other half spilled over her bare breasts. The little accident set her off again, and, fanning herself urgently as she gasped for breath, she went on, 'But it is not *possible*, my little innocent one! I'm a woman. I've been married a number of times. I know. It's not at all possible!'

But when the comic aspects of Mrs Barnfield's virginity had exhausted themselves in her mind, Toppateeter straightened up, and, with only a stray hiccup of mirth remaining, she poured more wine into the cups. She had another husband now, but on an occasion such as this he invariably found the most elaborate and far-fetched reasons for visiting his own people at that precise hour, and disappeared conscientiously after the midday meal, leaving Toppateeter free to enjoy the company of her son unhampered by the alien presence of others.

She thought of her husband's consideration, and was grateful to him; then, seating herself opposite her son, she sipped her wine daintily, and regarded him with half-closed eyes, so that she could remember each detail of his features, each change of expression on his face, in the long months that he would be away from her. Slowly her mind returned to the past, and putting down her cup, playing idly with her involved necklaces, she nodded her head vaguely, as if in response to deep, unspoken thoughts of her own, and became silent ...

When her son was a few years old, and the complexities of his temperament had already manifested themselves, she felt that he did not belong on October Island, that he would never be happy there. He belonged, instead, to his father's peculiar world that strange land beyond the Island that she did not know, and had no desire to know. At once, she began planning a future for him, one which, she hoped, would not only make him happy in life, but would reflect some credit on his celebrated father as well.

She felt that this was all she would ever be able to do for her son, and so it happened, when young Axel was scarcely six, that she took him to the American missionaries who were then resident on the Island, and implored them to teach him what they knew. As a result, the missionaries, whom he had never liked, began his instruction in spelling, reading, and speaking the English language. His mind was excellent, and he learned rapidly; and after he had been with the missionaries a year, they started his instruction in geography, grammar, arithmetic, and Bible history. He was baptized then as a reward for their labours on his behalf, in their particular faith, although he had long since forgotten what it was.

Toppateeter had always felt that the missionaries had not helped her son very much, and she was not displeased when they were recalled in the third year of the child's schooling. She wondered what her next move should be, how best to further her ambitions; but the problem solved itself not long afterwards when Wayland Yates, the anthropologist, and his wife, Dr Anna Reigenbach, the ethnologist, landed on the island for an extended stay. When they were settled, she took her son to them and told them who his father was, a revelation they received with widened eyes and polite expressions of surprise.

She asked them to teach her son the customs, and particularly the language, of his father's people, explaining that this was a heritage which she felt she had no right to deny him. But Dr Reigenbach, who was a gentle, plump mass of tactful complaisance, explained that Dr Hansen was Danish, while she was

41

German, and her husband, English. Neither of them had more than a reading knowledge of the Scandinavian tongues, but she did speak German, French, English, and Italian with some fluency, while her husband had not only those languages, but Spanish too; but if the boy mastered German and English, he would have no difficulty in communicating with his father, if later on they happened to meet, she said.

At that, Toppateeter called her son, who had been waiting unseen on the veranda, and when Dr Reigenbach saw the grave, polite, beautiful little boy with the vividly contrasting colouring, she had an impulse to put her arms about him and weep, for reasons she did not know herself.

'Oh, yes, yes!' she said eagerly. 'We will take him. We will do all we can for him.'

Later, they had both become inordinately fond of the child, and they taught him diligently. When they left October Island, they wanted to take the thirteen-year-old boy with them, but seeing the difficulties at hand they had parted from him tearfully, with embraces and protestations of love, with repeated and elaborate promises of remembrance . . .

Toppateeter sprang up suddenly and went to her kitchen, where her dinner was cooking slowly. A moment later she brought in an earthen pot containing one of her son's favourite dishes, which she had spent the afternoon preparing for him in the traditional manner. The dish was made of fillets of fish which had first been browned in coconut oil, and then baked with sliced coconut meat, rice, cloves, and a small wild onion that grew high up on the slopes of Min-Rahabaat. She brought in, too, a basket of fruit which had been cooling all day in the brook that ran nearby, and when everything was ready, and they began to eat, she regained her vivacity, and chatted on and on about the island and the things that had happened there since her son's last visit.

But Mate Hansen, although he smiled dutifully, and made the expected replies, heard little that his mother said, for his mind was concerned with other matters at that moment: Mrs Barnfield's story had stirred up old memories in him as well, and, as she had talked that morning, he had been tempted to speak of a disastrous event in his own life which had always troubled him, an event which even his mother did not know, an event which concerned his childhood too.

42

He had once had visions of meeting his father again, visions in which they were alone together in a quiet room. At first, they would only stand and look at each other, neither quite knowing what to do next; then, at the same instant, they would raise their arms and walk towards each other blindly, and embrace, their cheeks pressed together. Perhaps the old man would weep a little, laugh with embarrassment, and turn his head away so that his son could not see his tears of emotion; perhaps the boy himself would weep a little, too. Then his father would give him his bless-ing, and the boy would kneel, kiss his father's hand, and walk out of the room satisfied, without looking back.

This fantasy had so haunted his youth that later on he had contrived to be in a port not far from his father's home. At once he had written him an affectionate letter, a note in which he identified himself and expressed an intention of visiting him on a certain day, at a certain hour, to pay his own respects, and to offer the good wishes of his mother, who he said, was still well, strong, and quite happy.

On that particular day, he walked down the quiet European street where his father lived, stopped before the correct house, and rapped on the door. At once two policemen came out of the vestibule and confronted him. They thought it only fair to advise him of the punishment that awaits the extortioner, they said. He must write no more threatening or demanding letters; he must make no further effort to communicate with Professor Hansen in any way. Professor Hansen was a man of international reputa-tion, and of the highest possible moral standing; as a respected citizen, and a family man, it was only due to his sense of compas-sion and fair play that he, the boy, was thus given this second chance.

In those days, Mate Hansen had been a boy of sixteen, and he had listened to the policemen with a sort of shamed amazement. He kept saying, 'But what you say is not true at all. He is my father. How could I possibly hurt my own father?'

It had not occurred to him before in his fantasies, but all at once he knew his father was ashamed of him, and of the episode that had resulted in his existence – that he had cancelled both from his mind with cold and efficient calculation. When he accepted this hateful knowledge, he bowed to the policeman with all the dignity he could command, and walked down the steps;

but when he was on the pavement once more, something impelled him to pause and look upward at a small window, shaped something like a diamond, which was set just below the eaves of his father's house.

At the instant he turned and lifted his head, the curtain that covered the attic window was pulled cautiously back, and he stared for a moment into the eye of his father, an eye as cool and impersonal as the wary eye of God; then, suddenly, the eye was gone, and the curtain fell again into place, and he was alone in the world once more, as he had been from the beginning.

The memory of that bitter day remained with him all his life. When it was fresh in his mind, he would often stop what he was doing, stand still, and shudder; but now, eight years afterwards, he only felt shame, and a little regret as he recalled the senseless, unnecessary humiliation . . . He sighed, and shoved his plate across the table. In a way, now that he was more experienced, more versed in the cruel actualities of life, he did not blame his father for what he had done: his father had married again, and had other children whose lives must be considered, along with his own. Who, under those conditions, would welcome a forgotten, half-breed bastard?

He was conscious of his mother's voice once more, of her small, plump hand resting on his arm. What had become of his fine *appetite* she wanted to know? He was eating nothing, absolutely nothing at all! Could she pour him more wine? – it was quite good, really! . . . Perhaps a mangosteen would be nice, or even one of those little red bananas. She held a segment of mangosteen towards him, and obediently his mouth opened and received it.

When he had swallowed it, she said that she had something *really* nice for him this time: the dish which, as a child, he had esteemed above all others; and rising from her mats she went to her kitchen and returned with the delicacy she had promised: it was the meat of the makapuno coconut, served in its own shell. She had taken out the soft, custard-like mass, which was not much heavier than cream in its consistency, and had mixed into it wild honey, nutmeg, and powdered cloves; then, adding wine and a little palm sugar, she had baked the mixture in her oven until it was a golden brown on top. Her neighbour's children had searched all day for the makapunos, she said, and at last they had found three at the south end of the island.

44

As they had eaten their meal, Toppateeter and her son had set aside the choicer bits of food, arranging them on the *abalone* shells beside their plates; and when the meal was finished, they took their offerings and went together to the family shrine near the brook. They placed the food on the altar, and with lowered eyes they dedicated it to their god Rahabaat and his consort, the sleepy, top-heavy Kallapaaga; then, when these things were done, they knelt together, side by side, and said their prayers.

The sun was down behind Min-Rahabaat, and the whole western sky was washed with colour as they returned to the cottage and sat there in silence. The soft shadow of the volcano fell across the island, and into the sea itself, and Mate Hansen, surveying sky and volcano, rolled a cigarette for himself, and one for his mother. They smoked in silence, and then, as though remembering a thing of the gravest importance, Toppateeter made an excited, unintelligible sound and went into her cottage. She returned with the Hawaiian guitar her son had given her the year before. She said that he must now play and sing for her, but he took a deep, final draw on his cigarette, flipped it into the sand, and said he was not in the mood for music that particular afternoon.

Toppateeter pouted, agitated her bangles, and, resting her broad back against the canarium tree, she said that if her son would not sing for her, then she would be forced to sing for her son. She struck a chord and began a song in praise of Kallapaaga – an old song which the priests had once sung in the temple. Her voice was tremulous and off key, and as she sang, her son laughed affectionately and put his hands over his ears. When he could stand it no longer, he slapped her on the thigh and said, 'My God! My God! You get worse and worse!'

She wriggled like a delightful old spaniel as he took the guitar from her, settled back on his mats, and strummed it absently for a time.

'Play that old "Song of Arrival",' she said. 'It's the sweetest of all, I think.'

He nodded, smiled, and began to sing, his eyes half-closed, his head tilted back, his pale brown throat – a massive throat with a complexity of bone and muscle and triangular, supporting tendons – swelling a little as he sang. His voice was a small, liquid tenor of almost unbearable purity: you were surprised at so sweet a voice issuing from so powerful an instrument.

When the song was finished, it was time for him to leave, and he went inside the house and put on his white suit again. He returned and stood awkwardly beside his mother, and then, pressing his cheek against her own, he walked away.

Toppateeter had become accustomed to these meetings and partings. She would not see him again for six months; she would miss him greatly later on, but for the time being, she had other matters to engage her attention, for soon her husband would return, ravenous from his long walk; soon, she must take off her finery, go inside, and get ready the more average meal that she would serve him. Then, suddenly, as though something amusing had just occurred to her, she called out gaily to her son, and he stopped and rested his back against a palm tree.

'You are going in the wrong direction, my ardent one!' she said. 'The prettiest girls no longer go to the mango grove. They collect themselves now on the west beach, near the old wreck.'

He laughed, surprised that she had read his intentions so accurately. She advanced a few steps towards him, and continued, 'If you catch one, take off your suit first. You'll get grass stains on it if you don't. Young girls are all silly and impractical. They have no concern at all about a man's possessions.'

Then, as he laughed, nodded, and waved to his mother, she went again into gales of laughter, her shoulders shaking, her breasts vibrating, her necklaces rattling and clanking together.

He found the place where the old wreck was, and there before him were the young girls his mother had mentioned, the girls who, through the elaborate system of trial and error traditional to October Island, now sought their future husbands. They sat languidly on the wreck, outlined against the froth-topped waves and the soft, claret-coloured sea, or ran up and down the beach giggling, and catching fireflies for their hair.

The etiquette of these occasions was precise and long-established: the man, the traditional pursuer, was permitted but one choice on one particular occasion; and if the girl he selected found him desirable, and accepted his courtship, she put a flower in her hair to signify her acquiescence; but if she did not approve of him, or found him unattractive by her individual standards, she shrugged, and turned her back, and at this signal the other girls began to jeer and throw pebbles and sticks at the pursuer until he ran away in confusion. It was a precaution that gave the less attractive of the maidens a chance too; for before a pursuer risked the humilation of public rejection, he would first debate his own attractiveness to others, would calculate his chances of success with one of the popular belles, or the sought-after beauties, of the island.

Mate Hansen regarded the girls for a time, and then, having made his selection, he stopped before a tall, handsome girl and put his left hand on her shoulder. For a moment she regarded him in silence, as though undecided what course to take. Really, she found his light eyes and his flaxen hair slightly disagreeable, as though in bad taste; then, too, he was a little older than the other unmarried men of the island – he must be twenty-three or twenty-four, she thought – and his affected dress and manner were embarrassing; but she, herself, was almost eighteen, and she'd not yet found a husband of her own, and could not afford to be too discriminating; then, slowly, she raised her arm and fixed the flower above her ear; and leaping down from the hull of the wreck she ran up the beach with short, dainty steps. He followed her, careful not to catch her too soon, and a little later, when it was assumed by tradition that she was exhausted, and unable to defend herself against the ravening beast who would destroy her, she turned significantly into the underbrush, and waited.

A moment later, she called out shrilly, 'Kallapaaga! Kallapaaga! Oh, most divine, top-heavy Kallapaaga! Save me now! Save me from this impetuous monster who seeks my innocence!'

Her friends, hearing her cries of dismay, laughed appreciatively, and slapped at one another with their flowers.

A moment later the girl cried out – more loudly this time, so that all could know of her unwelcome plight: 'He has overpowered me! He is now destroying my good name!' And then 'Oh, divine, oh compassionate Rahabaat! Save me! Come to my assistance now, before it is too late!'

An old man and his wife, out in the twilight, wading in the shallow water near the beach to spear flat-fish, shook their heads in amusement, faced each other, and smiled at the theatrical exaggerations of the young.

It was dusk when Mate Hansen reached his schooner again,

and already, against the blue velvet of the sky, stars were popping out before his eyes. He undressed, and swam once more in the warm lagoon, listening to the muted merriment that came to him from the beach. He thought of himself, and what his life had been to this point of his development; he wondered what fate awaited him at the end. He thought, too, of his mother: he disapproved of her in some ways, in others, he found her absurd; but he loved her, too, despite her silliness, with that naïve, unreasoning affection that lasts for ever.

He returned to the deck, rolled himself a cigarette, and sat there smoking and stretching himself lazily. A full moon was struggling up above the blurred horizon, and he watched it for a time; then, overcome by his drowsiness, he threw his cigarette over the side of the ship and went below, stretching himself out on his bunk, his head cradled in his locked palms. At once he turned on his side, and thought idly of Irma Barnfield and her husband; but the images blurred and ran together, and in the middle of an involved thought which never revealed itself to the end, he turned again, this time slowly, and was deeply asleep.

Chapter Five

WHEN Mrs Barnfield was a little girl, and lived with her parents in Pennsylvania, her grandmother McCaleb had once told her that each day was like a treasure-chest of hours and minutes and seconds. These wonderful gifts were not granted us to be wasted, she said; instead, they were to be used thriftily, and with thoughtful kindness, and they were to be lived up to with such an undeviating earnestness that none of them was frittered away or remained unexpended at nightfall.

She had long since forgotten both her grandmother and the parable she had heard, but the effect of the story was to remain with her for ever – a part of her character, a pattern in her mind – so that even now she had a sense of uneasiness in idleness, a feeling of guilt at indolence; and thus months later, after she and her husband had made tentative friends with the natives, and Sam had already begun his first efforts towards turning them all into duskier Gospel Prophets, she found herself unable to rest for an instant, or loll back in leisure, and enjoy the beauties and ease of October Island.

The language had not been at all difficult to master. 'If you have a sound basis of workable Malay,' she had always said to new missionaries, 'The dialects come easy.' Sam, as usual, with his stern preoccupation with participles, had taken longer. Sometimes his stolidness, his slowness of speech, his strange New England ways, tried her beyond endurance, but she prided herself on the fact that not once in the long years of their marriage, despite the provocation she suffered, had she allowed the sun to go down on her unresolved anger, or failed to make those first efforts of reconcilation so necessary on the part of a wife who knew her duties.

From the beginning, the Reverend Barnfield had found his attempts at conversion disheartening. It was the first time in his career that he'd failed so completely, that he'd had no success at all, and he wrote fully on the subject to the Governing Board of Ordained Bishops, asking both their prayers for his success, and their advice as to future procedure. Slowly, he realized the difficulty that hindered him: you could save only those who were lost, who acknowledged that fact with lamentations and tears of remorse. The acknowledgement of guilt was the first step on the way to salvation, he thought; without it, he could accomplish nothing. Guilt was the medium he used in attaining his way, in reducing his congregations to that necessary basic desperation which made them tremble and cry out for God's aid as they contemplated the unending pain of hellfire that he promised them ...

But the October Islanders had no guilt at all. How, then, could they be saved, if they did not even know they were lost? How could their hearts be softened? How could they be turned away from sin? ... It was all most saddening, most discouraging; but he felt that he must not lose hope, that he must continue to struggle in the vineyard of the Lord and pray that some great, revealing incident turn them to the path of salvation, the path that he now pointed out to them.

He would come back from his calls in the Radja's village, or his incidental talks with strangers he met on the paths, and recount to his wife how, instead of listening to his words, the people had sidled away so imperceptibly that somehow they managed to melt into the brush, almost before his eyes. She would nod and say, 'Yes, I know, Mr Barnfield. But we must keep up the good work. We must not lose heart. Things will change.'

In the mornings, after her housework was done and she had planned their lunch and dinner for that day, she would get out her sewing machine and a bolt of the calico they had brought with them, and make the sack-like dresses which she hoped eventually to slip over the heads of her stubborn parishioners. She showed the garments to the women of the island, commenting on their perfection and making seductive noises with her lips; but the October Islanders would only look at them as though they were a cleverly concealed trap, laugh good-naturedly, and run away.

Often in the afternoons, during the warmest hours of the day when everybody else was asleep and living in unreal worlds of their own, Irma would faithfully practise hymns on her melodeon, or take walks along the shore to pick up driftwood for her oven, or shells for the flower-beds she was setting out beside the walk that led to her door.

Sometimes, she went into the forest to gather plants for her garden, and once, while deep in the interior, not far from the base of Min-Rahabaat, she saw a plant growing from the side of one of the small, rocky hills. From a distance, it seemed like a violet, and yet from another angle it was plainly too large, too brilliantly coloured, for any violet she had ever seen; nevertheless, it was as close to a violet as any plant in this land of heat, brilliance, and immodesty could reasonably be expected to be, and at once she wanted it for her garden.

The roots of the plant went deeper than she had thought. They were laced about a small, elliptical stone, and she dug out both stone and roots together; but when the violet was safely in her hands, the stone fell away from the dirt and lay obscenely in the sunlight; beside her feet. She stared at it in disbelief, being unable at that instant to credit its shocking, hermaphroditic frankness.

She would not touch the stone with her hands again, but she turned it over with the toe of her boot, got down on her knees, and studied its flat, smooth sides; then, shrouding one hand in her skirt, she grasped the stone by the end that depicted a breast, and buried it in its original place. She dusted her hands and hurried away, saying indignantly, 'Who would have thought that such *nastiness* could be hidden behind a violet?'

The unpleasant incident, which ordinarily she would have dismissed from her mind, made an odd impression on her, and that night, as she lay in her bed, she saw the image again in all its lewd significance. The surfaces of the stone were even and highly polished, and they were covered with faint but quite legible characters. She told herself that these characters were merely the marking of time and erosion, or, at best, the meaningless scribbling of an ancient October Islander who had no better way to employ his time; but she could not make herself believe these things, for in her heart she knew that the markings on the stone were the written words of thousands of years ago, and that they had been put there for a purpose, by some patient and highly skilled hand.

There was a set of encyclopedias among the books that the archaeologists had left behind, and since she knew she was now too disturbed to sleep that night, she got up, lit a candle, and turned to *October Island* in the index, not really expecting to find a place as obscure as it was mentioned at all. To her surprise, the island was not only mentioned by name, but there was column after column of print devoted to its remote and most remarkable history.

She read on and on, discovering that the island's name, which she had taken for granted as being the identifying month of its discovery by some courageous adventurer, was, in reality, a corruption of the far older title Ok-tur-baat, which was believed by Professor Hans Axel Hansen to mean 'Garden of the Eternal Breast', or, alternatively, 'Garden of the Final Redemption'; or even, according to the dissenting reading of Reginald Sykes, 'Place of the Beginning and Ending', or, more simply, 'The Earth'.

But regardless of the scientific battles that had been fought over its name, October Island was now generally considered as being the site of the world's great culture – a sort of pagan Garden of Eden where Shurabast, that cult dedicated to the worship of the hermaphroditic god Rahabaat, had originated some ten to twelve thousand years before the birth of Christ.

At its peak, Shurabast had been world-wide in scope, and, in the opinion of Anna Reigenbach, it had changed the direction of all early beliefs, and had influenced, at least indirectly, the great religions of the mainland that were destined to supplant it in power. Then, gradually, its strength had abated until at length its rituals were observed only on the island of its origin, and even there, according to Professor Hansen, in only a rudimentary and inconclusive form.

Some authorities, notably Professor Johannes Grots, and Dr Clement Higgs, were of opinion that the priests of Rahabaat had perfected the first alphabet, and had passed it on to the barbarians of the mainland. The evidence on which their position rested was controversial in the extreme: to some, it was as convincing as evidence could be; to others, it was inconclusive at best, or without true scientific substance. Some of this disputed evidence was as follows:

In one of the earliest known Sumerian bas-reliefs, there was depicted a priest of Shurabast with a scroll in his hand, to which he was pointing significantly; in early oriental writings, and in the legends of many of the peoples of the Pacific islands, there were references to the palm-leaf scrolls that the priests of Shurabast had once sent as epistles to their outlying, parochial churches, a custom which, it was thought, had given birth to the otherwise senseless aphorism of the Orient, 'Dispute not the written word of Shurabast'; then, too, in one of the few fragments of the early poet Kappadorus which have survived, there occurs the line, ' . . . thus let me be as changeless as the graven word of Shurabast.'

There was, as well, the ancient story of the Chinese merchant who had swapped his daughter, a girl of unparalleled virtues, for a prayer-stone from October Island, saying that while his daughter had all the excellencies possible, the prayer stone was definitely less boring.

But the most convincing of all the evidence that writing had once existed on October Island, one which came into our own day historically, was from Alexander Gillies, the eccentric Scottish traveller of the seventeenth century. He was said to have been the first European to set foot on October Island, and while there, as he reports in his memoirs, he bought a most peculiar stone from one of the natives. The stone was covered with minute writing, and he had kept it a while as a pornographic curio, but since Mr Gillies had been a bored traveller, and not a scholar, he had had no idea of the scientific importance of his purchase, and not caring to have it found among his effects in case of sudden death, he had tossed it one day into Southampton Harbour . . .

Several expeditions, notably the ones of Johannes Grots and Muriel Hawkins, had gone to October Island to seek out the writing, but without success; but if these claims could be supported with positive evidence, if October Island had actually possessed an alphabet, and had preserved some written record of its civilization, then it was plain that many of the sciences, and much of the history of man's eternal struggle upward, would have to be rewritten, or repudiated in part.

The article ended with a description of Min-Rahabaat. It was situated near the Island's one harbour, a few miles back from the coastal plain. It was thought by the natives to be the home of Rahabaat himself, the god occupying the right cone, his enormous top-heavy wife Kallapaaga dwelling in the cone to the left.

When she had finished her reading, Irma went back to the bedroom and stared thoughtfully at her husband. He was deeply asleep, his mouth opened a little, his stringy, greying legs exposed as high as his thighs. She sighed patiently and pulled down his nightshirt, blew out her candle, and lay primly in her own bed. The article had both disturbed and frightened her, and she was glad now that she had not told her husband about the stone, as she had been tempted to do at supper. His temperament was different from her own, and he would have insisted, in his plaintive yet stubborn voice that the stone, no matter what its implications were, be sent to a museum for study, and perhaps eventual deciphering.

At that moment she had a sense of jubilation, a quick feeling of triumph over the scientists who had sought methodically and failed, when she, by chance, had succeeded so decisively. She turned on her side, wondering if by any possible stretch of the imagination the stone contained matter at variance with her individual, specialized beliefs. She got up and walked about the room. It was not that her own faith was too weak to withstand some foolish, heathen doctrine, she thought scornfully. That was not the issue at all. She was sure of herself, and what she stood for – but were the faiths of others equally strong, equally rooted in the great rock of divine conviction?

If the object she had found was a prayer-stone, as she knew of course that it was, something prepared by the priests of Rahabaat, and sold to their followers, then the hill itself was a priestly post office, a place where the worshippers had buried their petitions with the naïve trust of children sending letters to Santa Claus up a chimney.

She considered these matters for a long time, and then with one hand pressed in perturbation against her cheek, she decided that she would do nothing for the moment : she would wait and see what the passing of the weeks revealed to her. She would wait and see ... But the next morning she went again to the hill where she had reburied the stone, dug it up, washed it, wrapped it in a piece of cloth, and hid it at the bottom of her trunk.

She determined to forget the prayer-stone and its lewdness, and she turned again to her sewing machine and her bolts of calico; but she worked with no great enthusiasm, for she was a little disheartened at her lack of success in clothing her flock. Then, as she worked, she had a brilliant idea, and as soon as it came to her mind, she was surprised she had not thought of it sooner : she had not called on Toppateeter, although she had promised herself many times to do so; but if anybody were to wear her dresses, which were accumulating distressingly in piles beneath the thatch of her attic roof, she was the logical one to begin with.

She wrapped one of the dresses, one of her red number fours, in paper, and that afternoon she went to make her call. She found the cottage without difficulty, and Toppateeter, who had finished her housework, was just stretching herself out for an afternoon's nap. She welcomed Mrs Barnfield warmly, saying that the children were playing on the beach, and that her husband was in the hills that afternoon making sago. Her son Anol had spoken of Mrs Barnfield when she had last seen him, and in the very highest terms, too.

'Mr Hansen is a fine young man,' said Irma enthusiastically. 'So simple and unspoiled. Both Mr Barnfield and myself are quite fond of him.' She waited, weighed her words, and went on, 'He's a bright young man who wants to make something of his opportunities, and I confess I lost my heart to him in Honolulu when I saw him standing, so grave and handsome, beside the gangplank of the *Mattie B.*'

At her words, the remnants of Toppateeter's uncertainty vanished, and she talked enthusiastically of her son, and his wonderful qualities. He never forgot his mother, she said, rolling her eyes from side to side. He was as thoughtful a son as any woman could want. She showed Mrs Barnfield the musical box he had recently brought her, the latest in a series of gifts. He had once given her a picture of himself, she said, and getting the likeness from the chest where she kept it, she proudly exhibited it to her visitor.

It was the posed, comic photograph indulged in by lonely travellers both to establish their whereabouts, and to give pleasure to those left behind. There was a wide, eerie backdrop painted to resemble a jail, with *Greetings From Mobile, Alabama* lettered at the top. Below, there were three windows whose rigid iron bars were actually rubber. Mr Hansen's head was sticking through the middle window, the bars of which he was bending back with his hands. The heads of his companions protruded through the windows to right and left, and beneath the photograph were the words, in Gothic script, *The Jail Here Is Easy.* All the young men wore monocles, supplied no doubt by the photographer. Each held a lighted cigar between his fingers. Each was smiling genially, and each was plainly a little tipsy.

Toppateeter, as though she could never get enough of the picture, took it to the window when it was returned to her, and held it to the light, touching it lightly with her finger.

Mrs Barnfield said, 'Since you admire your son so much, you must also respect his *opinion* . . . Now, in some ways, Mr Hansen is closer to me than he is to you – he wears *clothes*, I mean, the same as I do. He has travelled widely, and has naturally met a number of ladies, all of whom wear clothes, too.'

Toppateeter looked up in surprise. 'Do *all* ladies wear clothes in the outside world?' she asked. It was a point which had not occurred to her before, and she had always imagined vaguely that clothing was the particular whim of the missionary.

'All *true* ladies wear clothes,' said Mrs Barnfield emphatically. 'All *true* ladies are fully clothed on all occasions, I assure you.'

She waited to let her point sink in, and then went on: 'How do you suppose dear Mate Hansen *feels* when he returns home and sees his own mother stark naked – or very *nearly* so!'

'I don't know,' said Toppateeter. 'He never mentioned it one way or the other.'

'Anyway, don't you think it would be more pleasant for him to find his dear mother fully *dressed*?'

'Maybe so,' said Toppateeter. 'I never asked him.'

At that moment, Mrs Barnfield unwrapped her parcel and displayed the dress she had brought with her. 'The point we're discussing was in my mind when I came to visit you this afternoon. To be perfectly frank, it was one of the reasons that prompted my call. Now, Toppateeter, won't you consider wearing the dress as an example to the other women of the island, and as a compliment to your son?'

All at once Toppateeter was her old self once more. She leaned back in her chair, laughing loudly, and said, 'You leave it. I'll wear it.'

She stood in docility while Irma slipped the dress over her head, and buttoned it firmly down the back. It was a little tight, she thought critically, but all in all it wasn't too bad a fit, since she'd never seen Toppateeter at close range before, and had selected it from her piles by guess-work; but Toppateeter, she must remember in future, took one of her number fives.

She was surprised at Toppateeter's acceptance of the dress. It was a triumph she hadn't looked forward to so promptly, and she congratulated herself on her cleverness in getting her way. It proved again that with faith and patience all things are possible. But she was to be even more surprised next morning when the Radja's three wives called at the parsonage and asked shyly if they, too, could have dresses like Toppateeter's.

Mrs Barnfield got up with alacrity, and went to her store-room, picking over the costumes she had completed until she found the colours and sizes her converts desired. They had hardly disappeared down the path before a group of six other women took their places, and that afternoon her store-room was filled with the gay, giggling women of October Island who had come to her to be clad. 'It's simply a miracle, Mr Barnfield,' she said later on. 'I didn't dare hope for success so quickly.'

She went back to her machine, sewing from morning to night; then, being tired from her efforts, and wanting a little recreation, she took a walk down the beach at sunset one day, and there, parading up and down, were the women she had clothed. The dresses were all neatly buttoned from their high, tight collars to a point below the waist. From the rear, the sight was most heartening, but, as they turned, Mrs Barnfield saw that great holes had been cut in the garments, and that the breasts of the women hung down outside the cloth as proudly, as arrogantly, as before. She sighed and pretended not to notice, although she was greatly discouraged. She hoped, in time, that the women would cover their breasts, too, would wear garments as modest as her own, but that was never to come about, for a few weeks later they all discarded their dresses, almost at the same instant. It had been a fad, after all, and it had run its course like any other; and having once exhausted itself, it was dead – if not for ever, at least for the generation that had produced it.

'Oh, dear! Oh, dear!' she thought. 'I'll never get clothes on them again. I might just as well go home and put my sewing machine away.'

She came up the path deep in thought, sighing a little as she walked. Sam was standing idly on the terrace, staring at Min-Rahabaat. It was late afternoon, and the volcano was shrouded in pearly clouds that drifted southward. The volcano with its fleecy white clouds put him in mind of a talipot palm in flower. He had seen such a palm in Java, with the area beneath it covered with the fragrant white blossoms that rained down softly from the gentle fountain at the top of the tree. The talipot blooms but once, at the end of its useful life, and then quickly goes back to the mysterious elements from which its perfection was created, so that blooming and dying become the same thing in its existence.

Perhaps he too, who had accomplished none of the things he had once hoped to accomplish, would in the end, if God granted him mercy, be like the talipot and perish in one quick, magnificent flowering that men could remember after his death. He turned, and, seeing his wife approaching up the path, he went to meet her.

Once, he had wished that she combine more depth of spirit, more tolerance of heart, with her admirable practical nature, but he now knew these things were not possible for her, and he no longer expected more than she was capable of giving; but she knew less about his true nature, he felt, than the most casual, unkempt stranger in a mission, or the occasional passenger he met on some coasting steamer. He sighed, raised his hands and thought, 'We must accept these things with grace. We must not complain.'

When he entered the ministry, he had taken a vow of chastity, although that was not required of him, and now, in an effort to be just, he counted the advantages of a union with his wife Irma, and knew that one of its blessings was the fact that this rather masculine, aggressive, literal woman would never, with her skinny body, her flat chest, and her freckled hands, tempt him from that vow.

Chapter Six

THE *Mattie B. Powell* returned in December, a few days before Christmas, and Mrs Barnfield, looking down from her ornamental veranda, saw her sails moving precisely behind the palms that grew on the beach below, as she came up slowly, tacked, and entered the lagoon. She wanted to go at once to the harbour to welcome Mate Hansen, but condemning such impulsiveness on her part, fearing that it might be misconstrued by others, she wrote him a note instead, inviting him to call at his convenience and see her new home.

Later on, the Reverend Barnfield went to the harbour to pick up their mail, to arrange delivery of the supplies on board for them. He took the note with him, and when he returned about noon, he said the schooner would remain in port several days this time; that the captain had given Mr Hansen the following afternoon off, and that he'd be glad to call at three, if that was agreeable to his hostess.

Sam had with him, tucked under his arm, a packet of newspapers and magazines, along with the letters they had received. He sorted the letters, and passed on to his wife those intended for her. She went through them quickly, wondering from whom each could be, but paused before a square, official envelope addressed:

Personal and Confidential

> Mrs Irma H. Barnfield
> October Island
> via Honolulu, Hawaii.

The letter was postmarked New Orleans, and she said under her breath, 'Why, this must be from the Chief of Police. It's the answer to my letter about Lurline.'

She opened the letter quickly, and saw that there were many pages of writing in a small, flowing hand with elaborate capitals and t-bars like miniature lightning bolts; and fearing somehow that the impact of the letter might be too overwhelming, Mrs Barnfield went to her usual place beneath the nutmeg tree, sat on a bench there and read:

Dear Madam,

Yours of recent date requesting information about Miss Lurline Huffstetter was received, and contents duly noted. I remember Miss Lurline very well, and have good reason to: Miss Lurline was the only person, man or woman, who ever whipped me in a fair, stand-up, bare-fisted fight.

Now, Mrs Barnfield, this is the way it happened: I was a young cop in those days, just on the force, and a complaint came in from Jackie Mason's place that Miss Lurline, who was working there at the time, was drunk and making trouble. It all started off by your sister striking one of the other girls whom she'd accused of stealing a rouge pot from her. Then she got madder and madder, when she thought how everybody picked on her, and started throwing furniture around. The landlady and the other girls took shelter in the front parlour, after locking and bolting all the doors, and when we came up the front steps, the landlady, who had a scared look in her eyes, whispered through the shutters, 'You better be careful. She's been smoking loco weed again.'

Well, Mrs Barnfield, Patrolman Bissonet had gone with me to make the arrest, and when we got to the front entrance, he said, 'I'll just stand here and watch the door. You go in and make the arrest. It's nothing but a girl full of hop.'

What I didn't know was that he'd seen Miss Lurline in action before, and so he deliberately took advantage of my youth and innocence. Well, to make a long story short, when I went inside the place, there was Miss Lurline leaning against the wall, waiting for me.

'You might as well make it easy on yourself,' I said. 'You better come along peacefully, and not make trouble.'

Patrolman Bissonet laughed and slapped his leg when I said it.

'You hold every card in the deck,' said Miss Lurline. 'Why don't you go back to the station house and leave decent people alone.'

'Listen,' I said. 'The patrol wagon is backed up to the door, and I'm going to put you in it. Are you coming willingly?'

A group of people had gathered at the door, and Patrolman Bissonet didn't make any move to shove them back, like he would have done ordinarily. It looked like he was enjoying the whole thing, and I wondered what had come over him.

'You wouldn't say that if you weren't a cop with the police force to back you up,' she said.

I was getting sore by this time, with Patrolman Bissonet snickering, and the crowd staring in and watching my every move, and I said, 'I'd say it no matter what I was. I can put you in that wagon any time I want to, lady! And that's what I'm going to do right now.'

'Take off your shield, flat-foot,' said Miss Lurline with a fishy look in her eye. 'Take off that shield, and let's see who puts who in what.'

Patrolman Bissonet laughed heartily at this, and so did the other Basin Street characters around the door. What I didn't know at the time was the fact that this was a sort of gag the boys had cooked up for me. They'd had experiences with Miss Lurline before, and I hadn't. They told me afterwards, the reason they did it was because I was getting too cocky and full-of-myself around the station house, and they intended taking me down a peg. Well, Mrs Barnfield, they did.

I took off my shield and put it in my pocket. 'My shield's off,' I said. I went over to your sister, and tried to take her around the waist, but before I could even touch her, that girl shifted – I never saw such foot-work in my life – and rocked me back on my heels with a straight left to the jaw.

'Lay your billy on the hall table,' she said.

I was real mad by that time, but I did that too, and said, 'My billy's laid down.'

Then I waded in, trying to land one on her button, and put her out quick, but before I knew what was happening, she came up with a quick right, and a quicker left, and there I was lying against the wall, and pretty groggy at the time, too. I got to my feet finally, shaking my head, and then Patrolman Bissonet, and the driver of the wagon, came in to help me. Well, Mrs Barnfield, after a few minutes we got the cuffs on your sister, and put her in the wagon. I'll say one thing for her though: she fought like a man. She didn't spit, kick, gouge, or pull hair; and when she knew she was overpowered, not by one cop but by three, she just sat there in the wagon, with that terrible look in her eyes, and said, 'I hate everything that wears pants!'

Below, on the path that ran near the beach, a group of young native girls were passing. When they saw Mrs Barnfield, they waved gaily and called to her, and Mrs Barnfield, a little dis-traught, waved back absently, 'Well, I never!' she said. 'I learn new things all the time.'

The story of her virginity had got all over the Island by now, and everybody had laughed over it, and wondered. They had invented a name for her which they called her behind her back: *Luala Mananola*, which meant, 'the one too slippery to be caught.'

When the native girls had passed, Mrs Barnfield took up the letter again and finished it rapidly.

The chief of police did not know how much information his correspondent had concerning her sister, but since she'd stated in her letter that she'd not heard from Lurline in more than twenty-five years, he would take the liberty of giving her the benefit of what the police blotter showed, as well as the information he'd been able to dig up himself.

In an aside, he stated that the old timers, including himself, missed Lurline, and talked about her at the precinct station when things were quiet. There didn't seem to be any colourful characters left any more – just mean wife-beaters, drunk-rollers, and petty thieves; then, coming back to Mrs Barnfield's request, he said that Miss Lurline had first married a river gambler named Blackie Mayford; but Blackie – and this was a matter of court record – had been shot and killed only a few weeks afterwards.

Lurline had next married a photographer, a frail little man who wasn't quite a hunchback, with a studio in St Peter Street, named Vetter. She was devoted to him, it was said; but he died a few years later, leaving her a little money, which she used to buy a bar on Decatur Street. The last information anybody had about Lurline was that she'd married again, this time to a man named Charlie Goodpasture, who came from Philadelphia, and had left town with him – apparently she'd gone to Philadelphia with her husband, and perhaps that was where she now lived.

He didn't have Miss Lurline's Philadelphia address, and hadn't been able to track it down, but he was a good friend of the Chief of Police there, and he was forwarding Mrs Barnfield's letter to him, with another letter of his own which requested, as a personal favour, that the Philadelphia Chief make a special effort to find Mrs Goodpasture and see that the enclosed letter from her sister was delivered.

The letter ended with a description of the New Orleans weather, and an appended paragraph which asked, in the event Miss Lurline were found, and accepted the invitation to come to October Island, that Mrs Barnfield be good enough to write him again, and let him know the effect Miss Lurline had on the natives there. It was signed, 'Respectfully yours, P. L. Eichelhorst'.

The letter made an unpleasant impression on Mrs Barnfield. She appreciated Chief Eichelhorst's detailed response, of course, and it was most kind of him to forward her letter to his friend in Philadelphia; but the Chief, she felt, was not at all clever, as no doubt he meant to be. His letter was the sort of detailed anecdote which, having been recounted over and over, had become fixed in its telling, had achieved a rehearsed clarity of both dialogue and pattern, with all the unities preserved, with the apt phrases precisely reproduced each time, and with pauses for laughs and questions, like a piece in the theatre. She intended to occupy herself with other matters, to put the contents of the simpering letter from her mind as soon as possible.

She returned the letter to its envelope, finished her other mail, and rejoined her husband on the veranda. At once, she saw that he was disturbed, for when she spoke to him he looked up and stared at her with that hangdog expression he had when there was something he wanted to confess, but didn't know how to go about it. There was a letter in his hand, which apparently he had just read, and she asked somewhat sharply, 'What is it, Mr Barnfield? Have you received bad news?'

He nodded unhappily, and said, 'It's about your father.'

'Is he sick? Is something serious the matter with Papa?'

But even before she asked her questions, she knew what the answer would be, and, seeing her husband's sad, serious face, she added faintly, 'When did poor Papa die?'

The Reverend Barnfield handed her the letter, and when she took it, he said, 'The Pastor wrote me, instead of you, thinking it would be easier for me to break the news.'

She nodded, held the letter tightly in her hand, and went with it to the kitchen, where she would be alone. Her father had died, according to Pastor Ragland's letter, serenely in bed, at the venerable age of eighty-two. He had merely retired one night, after his usual hearty supper, but the Angels of Heaven, envious of his Innate Goodness, his Militant Moral Perfection, had lulled him to rest with the soft rustle of their wings, and had borne him in triumph to Paradise, where choirs of Cherubim and Seraphim waited his coming with Lutes, Zithers, Harps, and Hymns of Praise.

The clipping that accompanied Pastor Ragland's letter was from the *Burning Bush*, a devotional weekly published by the Gospel Prophets for the improvement of their members. Its style, compared with the prose of the pastor, was pedestrian: it listed Brother Huffstetter's dates, and gave a detailed sketch of his life. Brother Huffstetter had occupied a unique place among Gospel Prophets, being the first convert their founder had made. It was a fact not generally known, but as a boy in his teens Brother

Huffstetter had lived with his parents on the farm that adjoined the Huhner place. On occasion he had worked as a farmhand for Mr Huhner, and he had actually been present in the field with his employer when their great founder had first seen Isaiah walking towards him down the rows of corn. The clipping concluded with the prophecy that Brother Huffstetter would be greatly missed, and that his place in the religious world would not soon be filled.

When she had finished the clipping, Irma went through the underbrush, and descended to a lonely spot on the beach that she knew. There, she sat down, put her face in her hands, and cried. She had always felt that when Papa died, her own life must come to an end, too; that existence would not be possible without his firm guidance; but after her first conventional rush of tears, she had none of the emotions that a loving, dutiful daughter should experience on such occasions. To her dismay, the only feeling she had now was one of relief, as though some enormous pressure had miraculously been lifted from her.

She tried to keep these horrid thoughts from her mind, but she could not; and then she knew her life had been arranged thus far not for her own happiness, but to spare Papa's sensibilities, and to avoid the quick penalties of his wrath. She had never had a real life of her own, had never taken any of those things which should have been hers by right – and all because Papa had wanted to keep her sweet and *unspoiled*, as he always put it. Even after her marriage, even after she was a missionary in the Pacific, thousands of miles away, she had had this unceasing dread of him, as though he could still reach out his hand with the strap in it and turn her into an abject, snivelling little girl again, one who, since she did not have Lurline's courage, must substitute hypocrisy instead ... But in her own whining way, she had always hated Papa as much as Lurline had! That knowledge was now consciously in her mind for the first time in her life, and once there it could never be ignored again. She wondered how it was possible she had not known these things before!

She got up angrily, tore the letter and its clipping to pieces, and scattered them along the beach, where the wind would blow them away. Slowly, all the rage she had stored up in her mind broke through at last, and her heart beat so rapidly that she felt as though she must surely faint; then, to her surprise, for she had intended no such thing, she threw herself on the sand and cried out, 'He's dead! He can't bother me again!'

Feeling as she did, she did not want to encounter Mr Barnfield at once, as he might offer her sympathy, and that, she felt, was the one thing she could not endure at this moment. She took a long walk into the interior of the island, her lips muttering the words she had wanted to say all her life, but had not. When she came back to the cottage Sam had prepared supper. Tactfully, he made no mention of her grief, and when the meal was finished, she went to bed on the rattan couch in the living-room and slept dreamlessly for the first time she could remember.

She woke refreshed the next morning. The past was over and done with, she thought, and she determined to put both her father's death and her own resentment out of her mind. She would not even mention the matter to Mr Hansen when he called that afternoon. She would focus her mind on more pleasant things, and when he came at three, she was, at least as far as anyone could see, her old self again. They went at once to the summer-house, and sat there discussing the things that had happened to them since they had last met.

Mate Hansen had brought with him a book which he thought she might like to read. It was written by his old patron, whom he had once loved so greatly, Dr Anna Reigenbach, and its title was *Myths and Customs of the Smaller Pacific Islands*. There was much material concerning October Island in it, he said. He was in no hurry to get it back, and she could go through the book at her leisure, returning it to him the next time he was in port. She thanked him for his kindness, put the book down beside her, and said:

'Speaking of *customs*, Mr Hansen, there's one question I'd like to ask you, and it's this: The women here have a certain outstanding – well, a certain physical *peculiarity*, if you've noticed what I mean. Both Mr Barnfield and myself have often wondered about it, and debated the probable cause. If you know, perhaps you'll be good enough to tell us.'

Mate Hansen raised his head and stared at the steady rim of the sea, a faraway look in his melancholy eyes. He explained that in the legendary past, when Shurabast had been all-powerful, the whole Pacific, and the known mainland, too, had been searched for young girls of such overpowering attractiveness that they were thought worthy to serve at the altar of Rahabaat himself.

When found, each novice was oiled, perfumed, decked with flowers, and sent to October Island, where, in an elaborate ceremony of dedication, she became the spiritual bride of Rahabaat, and the physical bride of his priests.

The present people of the Island were the random descendants of those voluptuous, carefully selected priestesses and their prurient but sacred partners; and no doubt the specialized beauty, the freakish proportion which had been the sole factor in determining the vocation of the mother, had been passed on with such persistence by her, that, in time, Nature had sanctioned the variation from average, and had fixed it for ever in the daughter.

Mrs Barnfield laughed in spite of herself, and said, 'Well! Well, now! Whoever *heard* of such a thing?'

Mate Hansen went on to say that since Mrs Barnfield and her husband had lived so long in the Pacific, perhaps they had been struck by the diversity of the plant life of October Island itself. It was a fact which had greatly interested the scientists who had lived there, among them his old schoolmaster Wayland Yates; and while nobody knew the correct answer to this phenomenon, Mr Yates was of the opinion that when the little priestesses left their native homes, they had been permitted to bring with them some flower seeds, some plant cuttings, some palm rootlets, some dearly loved fruit, to the fair Garden of Eden that was to be their future home; and while all the things so brought could not have survived, it was possible that many others had adapted themselves to the Island, had propagated, and persisted through the long years since that Golden Age of Shurabast's power.

He paused, and pointed in illustration to the right, in the direction of a tree which grew on the terrace below them. Only the lavender, umbrella-shaped top of the tree was visible from where they sat, and it trembled, strained, and raised its leaves upward under the perpetual breeze from the sea, as though it were a cloud too dense to lift itself over the lip of the plateau. He said: 'I remember the day that Dr Anna and I came on that same tree, on the west side of the island. It was just a tiny sapling then, and we dug it up together and planted it where it's growing now. Mr Yates, when he saw it, laughed and shook his head in amazement. He said it wasn't possible for that particular tree to be on

October Island; that it was a native of the West Indies, and found in no other place in the world.'

Mrs Barnfield nodded, and with a preoccupied gesture picked up the book Mr Hansen had lent her. She studied the title, her lips pursed a little, then putting the book down once more, she said in a somewhat plaintive voice that since the islanders were obviously simple people, one had a right to expect them to have simple minds, simple customs, and a simple language with which to express their needs. At first, she had reasonably assumed these things to be true, and had been taken in as a result of her trusting nature, for she had soon found out that the minds of the natives were not artless at all, but quite cunning in a harmless, captivating way; that their customs, instead of being simple, were, in reality, so complex, so dictated by tradition, that one despaired of understanding them at all; and in so far as language was concerned, there was not one to master, but four: the language men used in speaking to men; the language women used in speaking to women; the language men and women used in common, and the courtesy language for public occasions and for addressing strangers.

Mate Hansen rolled a cigarette slowly, making a vague sound of agreement with his lips. There was another language on October Island, the language that the natives used in communicating with their god and his consort, but since Irma did not know of it, after her months of residence there, he felt it would be discourteous to mention it now, and he remained silent.

Later, Mrs Barnfield brought out the fruit drink and the little pink cakes she had prepared, and as they sat eating and watching the hungry gulls, she tried to draw him out, to induce him to discuss his religious convictions, his purposes in life, his plans for making the most of the long years that lay ahead of him; but he shook his head, turned, and stared at her strangely with his long, grey eyes, impressed anew by her relentless kindness, feeling once more the trivial shallowness of her inbred faith. He wondered, at that instant, if the identifying mark of adolescence were not the easiness of its definitions, its garrulous familiarity with concepts that awe the imagination of the mature, and leave them silent.

She talked on and on, affirming, defining, and rearranging the articles of her belief. He was embarrassed by her sentimental fervour, and to escape her nagging examination of himself, to divert her missionary zeal to less intimate things, he began to talk of his early life on the Island, of the interesting people who had visited it in his lifetime. But she was not to be put off, and at last he said abruptly that he had no plans at all for the future. Perhaps it was just as well to have none; perhaps it was just as well to drift along quietly, and accept whatever came your way. If he had any goal at all, it was the acquisition of knowledge.

She laughed and said, 'When I was a young girl going to school, we used to discuss at big recess what we wanted most from life. Now, some of the girls wanted money; some wanted a kind husband, and a houseful of children – most of them did, really – some wanted to be writers or singers or actresses; some wanted social position; some wanted to help others in distress; some even wanted power, and the ability to command other people's lives. They used to ask me what I wanted, but I'd never say. I pretended I didn't know what I wanted, but of course I did quite well.'

'What was it?' asked Mate Hansen after a pause. 'What was it you wanted, Mrs Barnfield?'

'It will make you smile, I'm sure – it's so silly,' said Irma; 'but I wanted admiration more than anything in the world. I don't mean I wanted people to say, "Irma Huffstetter is a nice girl who respects her elders," or, "Irma Huffstetter writes a clear, fair hand," or things like that. I guess you could call what I wanted *adulation*, instead of just plain admiration, and I used to have pictures in my mind of people bowing down to me, as though I was a visiting queen of some sort. I suppose that was really power, too, in a way.'

She elaborated her theme, once she had stated it, and he turned and stared at her with such thoughtful intensity that she became self-conscious, and fidgeted in her seat. She wondered if he were becoming too greatly attached to her, if his friendship were in danger of passing the boundaries of good taste. She sincerely hoped not, for all she was prepared to give him, despite her admiration for him as a man, and the great pleasure she found in his company, was affectionate friendship; then, remembering how greatly her hair had been admired by gentlemen, this incredible woman arranged her scarf more modestly about her head, and tucked in the little tendrils that curved softly on her neck, as she did not want to be the instrument of Mate Hansen's undoing, nor cause him to lust after her in his heart.

She became animated all at once, and jumping up from her seat, she said she particularly wanted to show him her melodeon, which she'd mentioned so often on shipboard. He followed her into the living-room, and she went at once to the instrument, seated herself, and struck a few notes to demonstrate the richness of the instrument's tone. She said, 'Now that we're here, will you sing something for me?' He said that he would, and she added, 'Do you know any hymns? They're about all I can play.'

He laughed and reminded her that much of his education had come from missionaries, and that singing hymns had been a major part of it. He probably knew every song in the hymnal, if you came right down to it: as many, no doubt, as she herself knew.

The Reverend Barnfield came to the door and asked if Mr Hansen would sing 'Almost Persuaded'. It was his favourite song, he said, and he had not heard it sung really well in years. Mate Hansen said that he would, and Mrs Barnfield turned to it in the hymnal at once. She began the opening chords as her husband went back to the veranda, and seated himself in his chair beside the open window. He sat quietly, almost without movement, as he listened to the pure, sweet voice of the singer; then, turning a little, he rested his face in his gnarled, mottled old hands . . .

It was the hymn the choir had been singing when, as a boy of thirteen, he had joined the Huhnerites, so many years before, and the scene returned to his mind now with all its original terror. His people were all Methodists, and had not encouraged his going to the revival meetings that the Huhnerites were conducting that summer in the vacant plot back of McKesson's Hardware Store; but something in the unalterable harshness of their creed had appealed to something harsh and unalterable in himself, and he had gone night after night, when his chores on the farm were done, to listen to the sermons of denunciation, to shiver again at the everlasting agonies that awaited the sinner.

And then on that last night, when the doors of the church were opened to the lost for the final time, he had closed his eyes and thought, 'Can I stand the torment of hellfire for a minute?' He was sure he could. Then he thought, 'Can I stand it for two minutes?' Perhaps. He was not sure. And then came the final thought, 'Can I stand the torments of hell for three minutes, for a day, for a week, for all eternity?'

He knew that he could not, and with his body trembling in fear, with tears of repentance running down his cheeks, he walked down the long aisle of sawdust, and became a Gospel Prophet.

Chapter Seven

WHEN Mate Hansen went back to his ship, Mrs Barnfield picked up the book he had brought her, and, turning to the section relating to October Island, she began to read – first with indulgence, then with amazement, and finally with indignation, for October Island was involved in an unfamiliar and most elaborate cosmogony of its own.

In the beginning, if one were to credit the dogma of Shurabast, nothing existed but the sea and the sky. In the unmoving seas, there was only emptiness, but in the sky above there were Raha, the sun, and Baat, the moon – two deities of equal power, equal brilliance – who had strayed into the realm that is now our world, and had remained to warm it.

In those first days, the Sun and the Moon had wandered at will in the sky, over the world we now call our own, and into the unknown outer spaces that lie beyond; but they were careful not to approach each other closely, for the nameless power who had created them, a power so lost in mystery that neither Raha nor Baat knew his name, nor what he was, had prophesied that when these two children of his mind, who seemed so alike superficially, but were so opposite in reality, at last knew their differences, and came together in union, unpredictable things would take place; that the shape of the universe would change, and its direction be altered for ever, but whether for good or evil none could say.

And so the ages passed away, and then one day Raha felt himself drawn towards his companion, and, altering his course, he approached her, heedless, at last, of portents and prophesies. At first Baat was amused, both by the singularity of his structure, and the intense clumsiness of his purpose; and she laughed suddenly, and sound came into existence; then, since nothing that has issued from a god can ever be lost, the sound of her amusement still lives in the pulsating throats of birds, the gay ripple of water, and the liquid sound of flutes and strings. Her eyes filled up with the tears of her mirth, and she tossed her head from side to side; and the drops she thus shook into space became fixed there as stars that still keep the merriment of the twinkling eye that bore them.

She called out to him, warning him to come no closer, but as

Raha disregarded her, and wheeled about her in swooping circles, she became alarmed, and fled before him, the noise of her terror, the wild movement of her celestial body, being heard to this day in the sound of alarm, the tremulous rush of wind, that the typhoon makes as it screams, lashes out, and hurls itself in fury across the Pacific.

For days they streamed thus through space, these burning, heroic comets, the pursuer and the pursued. Raha, being male, was intent only in fulfilling his desire, but Baat, being female, was, in the manner of women everywhere, interested not only in the pursuit, but in her unique desirability which had prompted it; thus she made the error of lingering above the spot where October Island now is, since that spot was the clearest, the most beautiful in all the wide expanse of ocean, to peer down into the water, to examine once more her overwhelming attractiveness.

The pause had been fatal, for at that moment the Sun seized her in the embrace of the impetuous lover, and held her fiercely to him; but the Moon, when she knew she was caught at last, struggled and wept, as women have done since time began, pleading that the Sun release her and do her no harm, reciting to him the legends of her innocence and purity as incantations against his desire; but he neither heard nor cared what she said, and, as she struggled in his embrace, the warm, holy milk of her breasts overflowed its springs, and fell into the cold seas, where it hardened into land; and thus it was that Ok-tur-baat was the part of the world first created, the genesis of Shurabast itself, and its mystical Garden of Eden.

'Well!' said Mrs Barnfield. 'That *really* beats the Turks!'

She went on with her reading, to discover that after Baat had tried out all her feminine wiles and found that Raha could not be diverted from his purpose, she plunged with him through space, her milk falling wildly into the seas and creating atolls, islands, peninsulas, archipelagos, and continents, depending on how long, how fiercely she struggled with her despoiler over each particular spot in the ocean; but at length, when it seemed that Raha was too powerful to be repulsed and that Baat was too strong to be taken by him, they completed their journey through space and returned to Ok-tur-baat, having created a new world, although, of course, they had not done so intentionally.

They paused again over the island, still struggling, still locked together, and then Baat, hoping to cool her lover's ardour in the water of the seas, plunged downward with him; but her intention misfired somehow, and on the bottom of the ocean, under the shadow of Ok-tur-baat itself, Raha conquered her at last, and made her his wife.

But Baat would not surrender even then, and as she sought in desperation to escape her ravisher, she pressed upward against the pliant, newly-formed land of Ok tur baat, so that the great twin cones of the Island are, in reality, only the imprint of her lifting breasts.

Some of Raha's seed were lost in the sea, and everything that swims, dives, rolls, or frolics there thus came into being; then, as Raha and his bride soared into space once more, his seed fell on the land so recently formed, bringing into life the trees, vegetation, flowers, and animals. Two of Raha's seed fell on the imprint of Baat's breasts, one on each cone, and they became Kaplinja, the first man, and Ellomeat, the first woman, from whom we are all descended, as everybody, everywhere, knows. Then, after the world had been created in all its variety by the holy milk of Baat, and the sacred seed of Raha, the Sun released his bride, and went back to his place in the sky, his lust satisfied, his male vanity appeased for ever, for although he had exhausted his seed in one great, epic romance, he had also created a world, and a god to rule over it.

Mrs Barnfield put down the book, took off her reading glasses, and said, 'Well, that's news to *me!*' She looked about her indignantly, her eyes holding something of the outrage her mind felt; but after a moment she lifted the book and began again to read.

Not long after her nuptial flight, Baat knew that she was going to give birth to a god, and she could not resist approaching Raha, and telling him this remarkable news. Raha listened patiently to her, but when his wife had finished, he said that the new god would, naturally, be male like himself; but Baat, who was equally proud of her own perfection, said this was not true: that the new being would be female, like its mother. The result was that both Raha and Baat willed powerfully to achieve their different wishes; but again, neither was weak enough to be defeated, and neither strong enough, in the face of the other's opposing strength, to win decisively; and so when the child of the

73

Sun and the Moon was born, it was neither one thing nor the other, being half male and half female; and since he thus partook of the nature of both his parents, he was called Rahabaat, or Sun-and-Moon-in-One, by them.

Baat, when she first saw her child, this enigmatic thing which had germinated so strangely within herself, feared that its father would compete with her for its affection, or would try through guile or force to entice it from her, and for this reason she put her infant in the volcano Min-Rahabaat, the place of its conception. But once hidden there with only her own eyes to admire its grotesque perfection, with only her own voice to whisper to it the soft, languishing words that floated up from her heart, she could not leave the child in peace. Often, she altered her course through the sky to pause above the volcano and peer downward, while the young Rahabaat cried and drew back before the intensity of her heat.

On such occasions, seeing the foolish Moon approaching, Kaplinja and Ellomeat would rush to the sea, to sink themselves in the cold water there until Baat was satisfied and went away. She was so faithful in her attentions to her child that she gave them no time to build a house, plant a garden, or even to examine each other in admiration and populate the earth with their kind; indeed, it was soon plain that unless something were done the world would quickly be crisped and destroyed; that the flowers, the trees, the birds, and all other created things would perish with the first man and the first woman. Raha did what he could to restrain his lovesick wife, to warn her of her destructiveness, but the silly, possessive Moon would not believe him, and could not be diverted from her course.

But one day when Rahabaat was older, when his mother's devotion became too painful to be endured any longer, he seized her and crushed her head in his hands. From her mangled head he took part of her skull and hid it away in the volcano as a symbol both of his power and the divinity of his origin; and after that the world prospered and became green again, and the dead Moon, only a ghost of the splendid being she once was, drifted alone in the sky with no light of her own, showing only the pale, reflected lustre of her murderous son. Sometimes she shows the undamaged side of her skull to her son, and sometimes as a reproach she turns the crushed side towards him, hoping

74

that he see and repent the evil thing that he did to her in his anger.

But his mother's self-pity was wasted, for Rahabaat, once free of her possessiveness, never thought of her again. He grew steadily in the volcano until at last he had the united power of the parents who had created him. When he was grown he wanted a companion of his own, and thus it was that he fertilized himself, being self sufficient, and got his wife, the great, lethargic Kallapaaga.

Mrs Barnfield blew her breath on her glasses and polished them with her scarf as though the things she had read were only the result of her faulty lenses. 'Why, whoever heard such foolishness?' she asked. 'Everybody knows how the world was made. It's in the Bible.'

She felt a wish to hurl the book into the trees that grew on the terrace beneath the plateau, but remembering it was not hers to destroy she controlled her impulse, turned a few pages with her indignant hands, and went on to read another of the legends – a story which, in the opinion of Dr Reigenbach, was many years later in time than those which related to the creation of October Island. It plainly dated after 9000 B.C., since that was the usually accepted date of the sacking of Rahabaat's Garden of Eden by the savages from the mainland.

In an explanatory preface she said that at the height of its civilization the gentle priests of Shurabast had lost all capacity to comprehend the structure of the barbarian mind that surrounded them; and that with a loss of the ability to understand innate evil their annihilation was assured. Even when their safety was menaced they would not believe that others sought their destruction, for they saw only the reflection of their own reasonableness in their enemies, and considering an attack on October Island too far-fetched to be credited, they made no plans at all for their security.

And so it happened that when the barbarians came at last in their *praus*, and on their great rafts – there were probably not more than a handful of them, according to Dr Reigenbach's estimate – the priests yielded in confusion, since they could not permit their hands to shed blood. Thus, the priests were tortured and slain, their priestesses violated and taken into slavery, and the treasure of the temples looted and carried away.

Those of the Islanders who escaped the general massacre that followed had done so by hiding in the caves high up in the hills and waiting there in patience until their gorged conquerors had departed. When they returned to their villages they found their homes burned, their loved ones killed, their temples razed to the ground, and the power of Shurabast gone for ever.

The legend itself, which in the opinion of Dr Reigenbach was 'a perfect example of the restoration-of-glory wish', was to the effect that when Shurabast was discredited everywhere, when its worship was at its lowest, when Rahabaat was the amusement of the infidel and stranger, a great, virgin priestess would appear on the Island with a symbol so plain that all would recognize it.

This alien goddess would appear twice to the Islanders, first with others, and then alone. In her final materialization she would be borne by herself, and if she were pleased with the Islanders, and they with her, the final act of the drama of Shurabast would be enacted and the priestess would lead her worshippers to a thousand years of glory and happiness.

The obscure phrase, 'borne by herself', had puzzled both Dr Reigenbach and other investigators. The Islanders themselves were vague on the point, knowing only that this was the wording of the original promise, but the High Priest of the island was of the opinion that the saving goddess, if she came to them at all, would come in the form of a great bird . . .

Mrs Barnfield would read no more of the myths, and she closed the book and put it away in her cupboard, having already determined to return it to Mr Hansen the next morning before he sailed; then, as she stood there in thought, her head pressed against her cupboard door, she felt as though she could cry with exasperation.

She had been called upon to bear too much in the past days, she thought! First, there was the unwillingness of the natives to accept the dresses she had so thoughtfully made for them, and, in particular, the sly trick Toppateeter had played on her at the moment she had thought her success assured; then there was the smart-alec, belittling letter from the police chief about her sister Lurline; next, the sudden news of her father's death and the re-evaluations it had entailed – with her new sense of freedom from his supervision, with the desire to stand now on her own feet, beholden to nobody; then there was the finding of the prayer stone and her dilemma as to how best to dispose of it; and now, finally, this disappointment in Mr Hansen, who, despite her open frankness with him at all times, had so misunderstood her nature as to think she would take pleasure in an obscene and sacrilegious book that ridiculed and made absurd the elements of her own faith.

For the remainder of that afternoon she went about her tasks as though she neither knew nor cared what she did; and when it was night, after she had washed her dishes and tidied up her house, she came into the bedroom and lay in her own bed. But she could not sleep for a long time for her mind turned and rushed about in all directions at once. At last, when she did sleep, she had dreams of the sun and the moon hurtling through space, locked in an embrace of lust so terrifying that the thought of it made her tremble and cry out as they fled shrieking and emitting sparks through the orderly universe that the Lord God Jehovah, and nobody else, had created.

She awoke with her hands trembling and her nightgown wet with sweat. She got up and sat beside the window watching the thin crescent of Baat's mutilated head. Then she remembered the writing on the prayer stone she had found. She got it from its hiding place, and under the light of her candle she examined it once more, her eyes narrowed, her lips puckered in concentration as she tried to guess the meaning of the words there ... Perhaps the stone contained matter as blasphemous as the things she had so recently read – as devastating, as corrupting in its effect as the silly legends of October Island!

She got up, dressed nervously, and walked the beach alone, trying to work out her disturbing problems, wrestling once more with her conscience and her duty. It occurred to her, for the first time, that her finding of the writing, where the more thorough scientists had failed, was neither coincidence nor the average workings of chance as she had so innocently supposed. It was plain to her now that God's intention had been miraculously shown her – that His eye had commanded her eye that morning, that His hand had guided her hand as she reached in gently for the roots of the violet. Had He intended anthropologists or antiquarians to find the prayer stone He had the power to so arrange it; but He had not, for He well knew that they would decipher the writing and publish its idolatrous contents to the world. He

77

had meant her to find the stone, and her alone, and she must search her heart now for His purpose.

She considered these matters for a long time, wondering where her truest duty lay, and then, as the land breeze freshened and the tropical daybreak was unbearable with the clangour and screaming of the harsh-voiced, beautiful birds, she dedicated herself to the performance of new acts of devotion: to the uprooting and destruction of the writing of October Island.

That morning she took the prayer stone, ascended the slope of Min-Rahabaat, and threw it into the crater of the god as though she were an offended sweetheart who thus, in pique, returned her lover's presents to him; then, having found her first specimen in the little hill, she returned there later in the day, armed this time with pickaxe and spade, hoping to find others in that identical spot; but she had no further success that day, and when it was sunset she went back to her cottage to prepare the evening meal for herself and her husband.

In the weeks that followed she demolished the hill with her energy. Her quest was successful, for by the time the *Mattie B. Powell* returned to the Island she had uncovered four other specimens there, all of which she washed, examined, and threw into the crater of the volcano. She called on Mate Hansen and had luncheon with him on deck. She wanted to tell him of her quest, feeling that if she could not confide in him she could confide in no one at all, but caution prevented her. After all, she reasoned, although Mr Hansen was a man of education and culture, a Christian like herself, he was still an October Islander by birth, with half his blood the infidel blood of that outlandish place.

So she said nothing to him about the prayer stones, although that was the subject that occupied her mind almost exclusively these days, limiting her talk to the commonplaces of her own and her husband's health, to the minor, and, as she believed, amusing incidents of their everyday life.

She felt quite pleased with herself, for she was one of those people who think they move through the world in a cloak of secrecy, that because the queerness of their actions is unremarked they are also unknown, forgetting, in their complacency, that always in life there is the lounging figure beneath the oak to observe, the inquisitive eye pressed to the tilted blind to appraise.

78

But if she had hoped with the trivialities of her conversation to hide her activities from him, if she thought that he knew nothing of what she had been doing in his absence, she was greatly misled, for his mother had repeated to him only the night before all Mrs Barnfield's current eccentricities. She had told him that the Radja and his advisers had been perturbed at first, wondering what Mrs Barnfield's purpose was in attacking the little hill with such singleness of purpose. They still did not know the aims of her mind, and all they had determined surely was that she was seeking some peculiar object and apparently finding it.

This in itself was not at all odd since October Island had been raked and spaded by the various scientists who had visited it in the past: the peculiar feature was that Mrs Barnfield desired to take nothing away, and whatever it was she found with all her labour she returned it conscientiously to Rahabaat, its rightful owner.

On the whole her conduct pleased the Radja, his advisers, and the High Priest of the Island, although they were still puzzled by such piety, such devotion in an outsider. They talked the matter over in council, and the Radja gave orders that she was not to be disturbed in her work, that the October Islanders were to show no curiosity as to what she sought, nor to question her as to the purposes of her search. Her true intention, he felt, would reveal itself in time, along with her true identity, and that was soon enough on an island whose civilization had existed since time began.

Almost from the first Mrs Barnfield had found her skirts and petticoats and binding shirtwaists a burden that impeded her work, so she fashioned herself a new costume, one which, if not so conventional as the old, was certainly more practical for her present activities. The new dress, which had so startled Sam when he saw it for the first time, was cut on the lines of a man's boiler suit. It covered her modestly enough, and buttoned at throat, waist, and ankles. She made a series of these uniforms for herself from the brightly coloured calico she still had on her shelves, and in the weeks that followed she could be seen daily as she darted about on her quest, a thin, wiry, aggressive old woman armed with her lunch-box, spade, hatchet, pickaxe, and the obsessive fury of her intentions.

Sam said, 'But what are you looking for, Mrs Barnfield? Why

all this energy and toil? Your actions have me puzzled, and I don't mind admitting it to you.'

'I have my reasons. You may be sure of that. I don't fritter away my energies without cause, as you should know by this time.'

'Are you looking for botanical specimens?'

'Botanical specimens were concerned with my search originally.'

'Is the purpose of your search a scientific one?'

'I imagine you could call it that.'

'Are you successful in your chosen work?'

'As successful as you are in yours, I'm sure.'

'Are you collecting souvenirs?' he continued patiently. 'Are you taking specimens of the island's minerals?'

'Frankly, I'm not.'

He put down the book of sermons he was reading and continued, 'As your husband I have the right to know what you're up to. That is my duty, and I request that you tell me.'

'It's quite touching, I must say.'

'Mrs Barnfield, I ask you for the last time to tell me why you spend so much time digging and searching. I think you owe me that courtesy, at least.'

'I appreciate your interest in me, even at this late date, Mr Barnfield; but I must inform you that I haven't the faintest idea of telling you anything about my private affairs. Is that clear?'

He got up from his chair and said sternly, 'This has gone far enough: I demand that you give me an accounting of what you're doing! I no longer ask you to confide in me – I demand it!'

Mrs Barnfield's laughter rang through the house. 'Well!' she said. 'Well, that *does* beat the Turks!' Then feeling her own anger mounting, she added, 'I suggest you mind your own business, and let me manage mine! Who do you think you are, anyway? Papa? ... I'm twenty-one years of age. I'm quite capable of handling my own affairs and making my own decisions. The sooner you realize that the better it's going to be for both of us!'

She stared at him angrily, her jaw thrust forward a little, and after a moment his eyes wavered and fell. He turned, went out on the terrace, and seated himself under the nutmeg tree. He sighed and raised his hands in the air. When his wife had made up her mind there was no point in trying to change it, and he had learned that long ago. He determined never to refer to his wife's quest again, and he did not.

When the *Mattie B. Powell* came to the Island on her December trip, thus ending the first year of Mrs Barnfield's systematic search, she had demolished her original hill, and had sifted its dirt so thoroughly that she knew there were no longer prayer stones for her to find at that place; but she had kept a list of her discoveries, and her score at that point was fifteen, including her original find.

On that particular trip she baked Mate Hansen a lemon pie, since she knew how greatly he liked them, and took it to him. She found him this time more silent than usual, and after some urging he said he was worried about his mother. He had seen her that morning under the Hernandia tree as she waited to greet him, and he had been startled by the changes that had taken place in her. She was listless and plainly ill – she had lost a great deal of flesh. He had gone at once to speak to her, but she had made light of the matter, saying that her stomach had been upset for some weeks past; that it didn't amount to anything, really.

He wondered if Mrs Barnfield would call on her soon, would keep an eye on her during his absence, and she promised she would.

Chapter Eight

THE following week, Mrs Barnfield, remembering her promise, went to see Mate Hansen's mother; but Toppateeter made light of her illness. It was simply that she had this little pain and had not been able to keep anything in her stomach, she said. Her son Axel had always been of a nervous temperament, like his father, and, in his devotion to her, he was inclined to exaggerate her slightest illness. Of course she had lost some weight – that was a fact too obvious to be denied – but she could lose a lot more and still be considered fat.

Mrs Barnfield said: 'Are you sure it isn't your conscience that's bothering you? If it is, I want you to know that I've forgiven you for the underhand trick you played on me about the dresses. I realize now that it wasn't of the least importance.'

At her words, spoken so earnestly, some of Toppateeter's concern with herself vanished. She clasped her hands like a pleased child, fluffed out her hair, and rattled her bangles wildly, her eyes gleaming with the pride of those who originate and see their ideas adopted by the crowd. 'Oh, no?' she said. 'That's not the trouble? Oh, no, not at all!' She got up from her couch and tried to walk about her house, but she was weaker than she thought, and she had to lie down once more.

Mrs Barnfield had not meant to say what she did, but hearing her own words she was surprised to realize that she meant precisely what she said. Her character must be changing, she thought in dismay – the stern rules of her behaviour modified – for the question of wearing clothes or not wearing clothes seemed inconsequential to her now. Perhaps the atmosphere of October Island was relaxing her ideals a little; but when that thought came into her mind she shook her shoulders impatiently and said under her breath, 'Oh, fiddlesticks!' It was simply that she now had more important things to do than put clothes on people who didn't want to wear them. Let these trivialities be managed by those who had not been earmarked by God for missions of individual piety, as she had been.

'My husband worries about me, too,' said Toppateeter proudly. 'He says if I'm not better by the end of the week he's going to call in a *brunga-brunga* and arrange for him to treat me. But I tell him it's only a waste of time. I'm sure to be better before long, and I don't want those *brunga-brungas* hanging around if I can help it.'

Mrs Barnfield returned home untroubled and promptly dismissed Toppateeter and her illness from her mind. In the weeks that followed she continued her quest for the prayer stones, working now between the cones of Min-Rahabaat, where the great temple had once been, but with no success at all, and then one morning at breakfast Toppateeter sent her an urgent message, and she went immediately, wondering what had happened, what new complication had entered her friend's indisposition.

A group of native women stood quietly under the mango tree, shaking their heads and talking softly together, but when Mrs Barnfield approached they fell back a little and averted their eyes. Toppateeter's husband was standing apart, miserable and not quite knowing what to do. She came up to him quickly, but when she asked in that unreal whisper which is heard only on the stage or in the sickroom, 'How is she? Has she taken a turn for the worse?' he sighed, and turned his head.

Mrs Barnfield, greatly alarmed now, nodded and entered the cottage. Toppateeter was lying quietly on her mats, and she was surprised at what a change a few weeks had made in the old woman's appearance. Her cheeks were sunken and her skin hung about her in dark, clumsy folds, like a badly-fitting boiler suit. Her breasts were flat and lifeless as though all energy had been taken from them. Her hair was matted and she had abandoned her ear-rings, her bracelets, her anklets, and her intricate head ornaments, as though she had lost her vanity at last.

She pressed Mrs Barnfield's hand, her eyes moving from side to side. She had not improved, as she had hoped: in fact, only a few days after their last visit together she had become so sick that her husband had sent for a *brunga-brunga* after all. When he saw her condition he had called in two of his fellows as consultants, and since that time they had treated her with all the knowledge at their disposal.

'Are you in pain, Toppateeter?'

'I was at first, but not so much now. The *brunga-brungas* give me a drink made out of leaves and roots, and that stops most of the pain.'

Irma sat down on the mats and asked what the diagnosis of the doctors was. Toppateeter closed her eyes in order that others could not see the terror in them, and, pressing her face suddenly against Mrs Barnfield's bony chest, she said the doctors had agreed, after considering the factors of her illness, that one of the small, vicious land crabs of the Island had crawled into her stomach, probably during her afternoon nap, when she was said to snore and hold her mouth open a little. Once inside her the crab was now snipping off segments of her stomach with its cruel claws and eating these tit-bits, which it admired greatly, at its leisure.

Mrs Barnfield said, 'But what are the doctors doing for you? Are they able to help you at all?'

The doctors of October Island, said Toppateeter, were cautious and old-fashioned, and believed in a conservative method of treatment. The opiate they had prescribed was not only to relieve her pain, she said, but to deaden the claws of the crab as well. They had hoped, thus, to induce such a drowsiness in the crab that it would loosen its grip on her stomach; and thus, when she coughed, as she was instructed to do at intervals, she would, if luck favoured them, expel the crab while it was dozing and unable to think clearly.

But this method had not worked at all well in her case for the crab had resisted the most powerful doses of the drug; and it was then the doctors had tried another method: they had propped her mouth open with little pegs and held a mirror not far from her lips, hoping the crab would see a fancied enemy and rush out to do battle with it. One of the native boys, who had mastered the odd hissing noise the crab made when aroused, sat beyond the range of the mirror and made his angry sound over and over; but this crab that desired her stomach was not only tenacious, it was wise and experienced too, and it could not be tricked out of its purpose.

As she listened Mrs Barnfield had a sense of helpless pity. She had determined to show no emotion, feeling that there was enough of that already, but now, impulsively, she bent down and kissed Toppateeter's forehead. 'You must not worry,' she said. 'Everything is sure to come out all right.'

Toppateeter nodded. But of course! She was conscious of that! She had complete confidence in her doctors and she was determined to do everything they advised, no matter how unpleasant, for she wanted to be well again when her son returned to the Island. She didn't want him to see her this way, so droopy, depressed, and thin. She was determined to struggle against the crab with a tenacity as great as its own. Then, too, Rahabaat would not really let the crab destroy her; he would interpose and eject it somehow, if not for her own sake, then for the sake of her son Axel, who was so handsome, so witty, so intelligent, so greatly admired by the girls.

She waited, and then went on with the other aspects of her illness: when the crab could not be dislodged through drugs or illusions, the *brunga-brungas* had resorted to flattery. They had knelt beside their patient, and, in a long, derisive dialogue, they ridiculed the crab's lack of discrimination. This was a woman of no real importance, they said: just an old, ignorant woman with a stomach famous for its tastelessness – a stomach from which all the juices and flavour had faded. They were surprised that a crab of intelligence would waste its efforts on an object so inferior when there were many young, tender, and attractive stomachs to consume; but again the crab would not be taken in by their guile, and it was then the *brunga-brungas* knew they must resort to force.

And so it happened, the day before Mrs Barnfield's visit, that the doctors, dressed in their concealing paraphernalia, and wearing masks so that relatives of the crab could not identify them and take revenge later on, had flogged their patient with sticks and whips while their assistants shouted, rattled gourds, and beat on pieces of tin. Toppateeter had borne the ordeal with fortitude, but the crab was courageous too, and he did not come sidling out of her mouth as they had hoped.

At last the doctors had gone away, promising to resume the treatment next morning; but in the night she had had a great bleeding, and her husband fetched the doctors again. They had left only a few hours before Mrs Barnfield arrived. She expected them back later in the morning, when they had refreshed themselves, but first she wanted to see her son's dear friend and talk to her about certain matters which were perpetually on her mind these days.

She paused in confusion and said, 'If the crab wins the battle, if I never see my son again, will you say to him the things that are necessary to be said? Will you tell him that I – ' But tears came into her eyes, her voice died away, and she could not go on.

Irma said, 'I know what you want me to do. I'll tell him all the things you want to say. You can trust me completely in the matter . . . But you must not worry so. It will come out all right. I feel it.'

At that moment the husband came to the door and said that the *brunga-brungas* had arrived, and Mrs Barnfield rose to go. Then, in horror, she paused and cried out, 'Are they going to beat you again? – Oh, you must not let them do that!'

But Toppateeter said the doctors had abandoned that phase of treatment as useless. They had merely come this time for another examination, to confer together, and to devise new methods for handling her case.

Mrs Barnfield went outside and stared coldly at the doctors, as though they were responsible for poor Toppateeter's plight; then, after watching their preparations for a time, she returned to her own cottage. She repeated what she had seen, and what Toppateeter had told her, to her husband, and he raised his hands in helplessness, and said, 'But what can we do, Mrs Barnfield? What can anybody do?'

It seemed to him that life was a most cruel and senseless thing, that only with the greatest resolution could one get through it safely, or bow in acquiescence to the will of God. He wished he had studied medicine in his youth, as so many of the missionaries were doing these days; but that opportunity had passed, and he must content himself now with working in the fields of pure faith.

Mrs Barnfield said: 'When I left poor Toppateeter, and saw those absurd *brunga-brungas* hovering outside, I was so mad I could *spit*! They had brought with them all sorts of fetishes and charms. Toppateeter's house is full of them. They've set up an image of Rahabaat in front of the cottage, but what they expect to accomplish that way, I'll never know. Then, this morning, they brought along a stone idol, and some crossed sticks, which are said to work wonders in these cases.'

'It's most disheartening, Mrs Barnfield.'

'When I was leaving, they carried poor Toppateeter out and put her under the canarium tree; and Brenan-Oan, the Radja's nice-looking young nephew who almost has a celtic cast of features, unveiled the most sacred relic on the island. It's said to be the thighbone of Kaplinja, who they claim was the first man, and Brenan-Oan's sole occupation is to guard it night and day. Kaplinja is a sacred person with the October Islanders, but what good that old, mouldy thighbone of his can accomplish is beyond me.'

The Reverend Barnfield made a disapproving sound with his lips, and shook his head from side to side.

'I don't know what to do,' said Irma, her palms pressed flatly against her cheeks. 'I can't interfere with what doesn't concern me, particularly since Toppateeter is satisfied; but it tears my heart out to see the mother of a Christian young man like Mate Hansen being treated with idols and mirrors and whips.'

Mr Barnfield reminded his wife that the natives of the Island had not had their advantages: they were only ignorant, superstitious savages, and she must try to judge them charitably. 'We're here through their courtesy,' he said. 'We have no right to interfere with their customs, no matter how distasteful we find them, Mrs Barnfield.'

All at once, at least a partial solution of her problem occurred to Mrs Barnfield: her father, as the clipping from the *Burning Bush* has told us, had, indeed once worked as a farm hand for the founder of the Gospel Prophets, and had actually been present in the field on that day of great revelation when Isaiah first appeared to him. He had seen the agitated corn, and had heard his employer's cries of dismay; and he had sped through the corn as fast as his young, plough-boy legs would carry him; and although he had not seen Isaiah, his eyes not having been chosen for such a sight, he had seen Farmer Huhner struggling with a phantom adversary, a struggle so fierce that a button had popped off the farmer's jumper-coat, and had fallen into the adjoining corn row.

He had thriftily retrieved the button, intending to return it to its owner, but when Farmer Huhner was conscious again, and related his vision – when the young man knew the significance of the things that had happened that afternoon before his eyes, he had asked his employer to give him the button as a souvenir of the struggle, and his request had been granted.

Her father had treasured the button for a long time, and had often shown it as a holy relic to the congregations he visited. Later, he had had the button encased in a silver locket – the

Gospel Prophets did not believe in the use of gold – and when she married Mr Barnfield, he gave it to her as a reward for her lifetime of obedience. It was now Mrs Barnfield's most treasured possession, and thinking of it, she determined to lend it to Toppateeter, to counterbalance, with its holiness, the pagan superstitions that surrounded the sickbed of her friend.

When she visited Toppateeter the next day, she had the locket with her. She explained its significance, its unique sacredness, and Toppateeter thanked her in a weak voice, and turned on her side obediently as Irma fastened the locket about the dying woman's neck.

The doctors were now preparing a treatment more radical than any they had tried before. They tied one end of a rope to Toppateeter's ankles, fixing the other end to the stout branch of a tree. They calculated height and clearance, and when these things were accomplished, the men who were to take part in the treatment stood at their posts, while the *brunga-brungas* explained to their patient that at the instant she was jerked off the ground by one group, and swung head down through the air by the other, she must cough as vigorously as she could manage. She promised to obey instructions, and then looking about her in terror, seeing all those who knew her so well, who loved her so dearly, assembled for the ceremony, she said in a weak voice that it was only at times like these that we realized how many friends we had.

Then, a moment later, she was snatched violently off her feet, and swung in an arc through the air; but although the doctors watched with care, nobody saw the crab emerge. They lowered the woman to the ground, and tried the experiment once more, but again they were not successful. On their fifth attempt, Toppateeter implored them to release her. They did so, and she staggered blindly, fell to the ground, and said, 'Not again! ... No, not again!'

When they had her back on her mats once more, the *brunga-brungas* said they had exhausted the known methods of treatment for those suffering with the crab, except one. That remaining remedy was to slit the belly of the patient with a sharp clam shell, and detach the crab by force. The operation had been performed many times, they said, but never with success, and each time it had been done the crab had managed to outwit his pursuers, escaping before the doctors could find him, leaving behind only the damage he had done.

But Toppateeter, all skin and bones, all tangled hair and wild, imploring eyes, shook her head stubbornly, and said, 'No! . . . It's enough! . . . If the crab wants me so badly, then let the crab have me!' Her husband, her children, and her friends came up and made a defensive circle about her. 'It's enough!' they said. 'It's enough!'

She asked then that they carry her to Rahabaat's altar beside the brook, and when they had done so, and withdrawn beyond the range of her voice, she rested her head against the stone and said:

'O, merciful and all-powerful Rahabaat, who, being both man and woman, understands the terrors of us all: I do not ask that my pain be lessened, nor that I be able once more to enjoy the sun and the sea, neither do I question the divine will, nor presume to understand the hidden intention.

'But I am weak and very tired, O, stern and compassionate father, O, gentle and loving mother, and the darkness into which we all descend is not far from me.

'I ask nothing for myself.

'I am a vain woman who has added nothing to thy glory. I have not always worshipped thee with devotion, my mind being diverted so often with silly matters.

'I care nothing now for pain and suffering, being well used to those things, but before I die, let me see my son once more. Let my body, for his sake, be stronger than the claws of the crab. Let it endure until my son returns, and I shall die blessing thy merciful name.'

When she had finished, she wept, and they took her back to her cottage and put her on her mats. She asked her friends to comb out the tangles in her hair, and to brush it until its lustre returned. She put on her necklaces, her anklets, her beads, and her hair ornaments. She returned Mrs Barnfield's locket to her, saying she no longer had need for medicine or charms. 'I will survive until he returns,' she said. 'Rahabaat has heard my prayer. I know in my heart he will grant it.'

But the ears of Rahabaat are old and deaf, and his mind wanders at times in confusion, and that night, after Mrs Barnfield had returned to her own home, as she sat playing her melodeon and thinking sadly about her friend, Mate Hansen's mother had her definitive bleeding, rolled her eyes wildly, and died.

They buried her in the manner the October Islanders had used for ages: after she had been washed by the old women, and anointed with oils and spices, they wrapped her in soft, brightly coloured mats and placed her body in a palm canoe which had been hollowed, for the dead, to an almost paper thinness. They covered both body and canoe with gaily coloured flowers, and when everything was ready other canoes containing the husband, the relatives, and the close, weeping friends towed the hearse to a place beyond the eroded cliffs, a deep place in the floor of the ocean from which nothing had ever returned.

Farther away, there was a whirlpool of the currents that rounded the island, and when the funeral party had arrived at the proper spot the High Priest cut the funeral canoe adrift; and then, to the sound of flutes, marimbas, gourds, and muted drums, the mourners sang hymns to Rahabaat as the canoe drifted with the current to the whirlpool, was spun madly about for a moment, and then disappeared there for ever.

Mrs Barnfield did not attend the funeral, feeling her presence would be inappropriate at pagan rites; but she watched from the side of the cliff, and when the canoe disappeared, and only the gaily coloured flowers swirled in the eddy, or drifted gently to shore, she wept, as we all weep, not for the victim, but for ourselves on the victim's bier.

The *Mattie B. Powell* was due to arrive in three weeks, and Mrs Barnfield, remembering her promise, was determined to be the one who first told Mr Hansen about his mother's death. She gave up her search for the stones during that time, feeling that if she were inland she might miss the schooner. Each day she stood near the summer-house that the anthropologists had built, and watched the horizon for the sight of sails; and, almost to the day she was expected, the *Mattie B.* came into sight. She waited until the schooner approached the lagoon, and then went to the wharf and stood patiently under the Hernandia tree until she had dropped anchor, and the gang-plant was out.

She went aboard at once and told Mate Hansen what had happened, giving him the details of his mother's death, and repeating those things that Toppateeter wanted her to say to him. He seemed so unconcerned, he questioned her in such a matter-of-fact voice, that for a time she thought him shallow, and without feeling.

He left her without a word, and when next she saw him, he was walking in the direction of his mother's cottage. She followed him, not knowing what his reaction would be. These silent ones, who made no display of grief, were sometimes the most difficult of all, and she wanted to be within reach, if he needed her.

She followed him softly, giving no sign of her presence, and when he reached the altar to Rahabaat, he stopped and stood there with his eyes closed, his face twisted in desperation. He fell to his knees before the altar, his mouth moving silently. She watched him for some minutes, and then, when she could stand the sight of his grief no longer, she strode out of the protecting bushes, stamped her foot in exasperation and said, 'Cry! Cry! For God's sake cry, and end it!'

He stared at her with confused intensity, and then, as he lowered his forehead to the altar, and obeyed her, she went back the way she had come, in the direction of the schooner, thinking, 'I always considered Mr Hansen a Christian, like myself, but that was my mistake. He is not. He is a worshipper of Rahabaat, and that is the one he turned to in his sorrow; that is the one who came first to his mind.'

She did not see him again too soon, feeling that he would now want to talk with his stepfather; but at sunset she went back to the schooner and called to him softly. He joined her on the mole, and they walked together down the beach. They sat on the trunk of a tree which had been uprooted somewhere, in some distant storm, on some unknown island, and had been washed ashore, at this place, for their convenience.

After a while, he said, 'I'm not coming back here.'

'Not ever again, Mr Hansen?'

'Not for a long time, anyway.'

'What will you do now?'

'There are places in the world I've never seen. I'm going to sign on a steamer, and visit these places I do not know. Maybe I'll see Rio again. Maybe I'll return to San Francisco, and stay there awhile. Maybe I'll go back to New Orleans, where you used to live, and visit there. But I'm not coming back here right away.'

She was silent a long time, and then in the tight, mincing voice we use to hide our tears, she said, 'You must do with your life as you think best. Perhaps your decision is the correct one. I don't know ... But if you do decide to come back, I'll be waiting for you, and my friendship will be the same as before. I don't give my friendship easily, but when I do give it, I give it for ever.'

He looked at her, and nodded gravely.

'I'm not at all like that wonderful Dr Anna Reigenbach, who writes books, and who is so much more accomplished than I am, in every respect,' she went on in a hurt voice. 'She pretended to be your friend, too; but I notice she went away and left you, when it suited her convenience to do so, and forgot you quickly enough. I'm not like that at all, and I wanted you to understand that fact, Mr Hansen.'

Chapter Nine

IN the late afternoons, after her tasks for the day were done, but when it was still too early to start her supper, Mrs Barnfield would sometimes go to the summer-house, and sit there in meditation. At such times she would stare outward at the sea, her lips pursed quizzically as though she pondered the milder aspects of the universe, one palm curved on her brow to save her eyes from the rays of the sun that glittered and shattered themselves against the waves in a shimmer of white radiance. Sometimes her mind returned to the past, and she considered the enigma of her sister, wondering what had become of her, what dreadful life she was now leading, what new depravities she practised.

It had been two full years since she had written Lurline, and now, methodically, she checked the explanations of her sister's silence. She came to the conclusion that Lurline had not answered her letter of forgiveness and invitation because the letter had somehow gone astray, despite the efforts of Chief Eichelhorst on her behalf; and once having accepted this solution, she dismissed her sister from her mind. 'There's no sense bothering myself further,' she said aloud. 'I did what I could. If the letter wasn't delivered – well, I can hardly be held accountable for *that*!'

But she was incorrect in her conclusion, for Lurline had got the letter promptly – brought her in person, not by the ordinary postman, but by a lieutenant of detectives. At the time she received it she was forty-eight years old – a stout woman with the lumpy face of a prize-fighter who had worked too often in his youth; the mistrustful glance of a seasoned police matron, and the unhappy eyes and bitter mouth of an old hack-driver.

It appeared to her these days that everything she had done in life had been inept, and without plan or clear intention; that only when it was too late to correct her errors, to retrieve the hours she had wasted, did she see the pattern of her life with clarity; and so looking back on her past it seemed to her that the years of her marriage to George Vetter, the St Peter Street photographer, had been the only happy ones she had known. He had been half a foot shorter than herself; there had been something obscure the matter with his spine, his head had been a little too massive for his frail body, and she had devoted herself completely to his welfare.

It was remarkable, she thought, how easy it had been to renounce her evil ways for him, not because George had asked it of her, but because she felt he deserved the best, the most honourable of wives. She considered him a great artist, and she, herself, the handmaiden of his genius. And thus, during this wonderful period of her life, she went about on tiptoes, a figurative finger perpetually at her lips, so that neither she nor others should disturb that serenity necessary for creative work.

He specialized in dogs, which he liked to photograph with sprays of flowers between their teeth. These studies were often enlarged and tinted for the admiring owners, and they brought him considerable acclaim among the bawdy ladies of Basin Street, who framed them in gilt, and hung them above their beds, so that in time a George Vetter dog study became almost the identifying equivalent, in their profession, of the marriage certificate in more usual walks of life.

Sometimes, although the customer saw nothing at all wrong with the finished work, George would stand aside critically and say, 'It was a mistake to combine roses and a French poodle. Poppies would have been better.' Or, 'No, I'm afraid it isn't right. I wanted a fluid line from neck to tail on this magnificent collie of yours, but it didn't come off, as you see. The whole thing's a failure.'

Then he would tear up the photograph before the shocked eyes of his customer, while Lurline's heart throbbed with pride, both at her husband's sensitivity, and the high standard of perfection he held for his art. She would show the customer to the door, whispering in reassurance, 'They're all like that! He's going to do it over again. Come back tomorrow about this time; he should have something really beautiful by then!'

He had trusted her in all things, he had given her his complete devotion, he had called her, often when they were alone, and sometimes in the presence of others, 'The rock of affection and faith to which my poor life is attached for ever.'

It had been a full, true marriage in every sense, and when he died, Lurline was so prostrated with despair and grief that she had neither eaten, nor left her room, for days at a time; and then solacing herself with the knowledge that George, who had always been so brave, who had borne his own afflictions with such courage, would not approve her conduct, that he would insist that she go on with her life as best she could, for his sake, if not her own, she shook off her sorrow, and bought a bar on Decatur Street with the money he had left her, feeling that, since she no longer drank at all, she should be in an excellent position to handle such an establishment.

The bar under her management did well, and for a time a young man named Charles Goodpasture had been her most profitable customer. Charlie had black, silky hair, which he divided precisely in the middle of his head in a wide parting which revealed skin of such dead whiteness that, in gaslight, it seemed blue. His eyes were a greenish-hazel, and they bulged outward a little, as though pressure were applied to his throat. He had stumbled into her place by accident, he confessed later, in one of his moments of relative sobriety; but once there, once having established himself as a pampered patron, he usually was first to arrive in the morning for the pick-up that would get him through those early, dreadful hours of the day. He knew from the beginning that there was something about himself that appealed to Lurline, that he could have anything he wanted from her, and, to show the less favoured his power over her, he occasionally ridiculed her to her face; but, planting her elbows on the bar, she would rest her chin on her laced fingers and smile fondly at him, as though she were his nurse, and was proud, in her individual way, of his robust cleverness.

She knew little about him, for in discussing his past he lied with a lavishness which seemed beyond his power either to correct or control; and listening to him night after night, as he sat drinking at her bar, as he glanced down modestly and smiled in propitiation, as though charm must take the arrogance from the words he had to utter, she got the composite impression that he was true heir to the Russian throne; that he was born in England, the illegitimate son of the Duke of Westonshire and Lady Agatha Farquaharson, the most famous beauty of her time; that he was in New Orleans to forget a famous actress, whose name he was too much the gentleman to mention 'in a place of this sort' – an intense lady who had attempted suicide when he spurned her attentions; that he was of straight American stock, and proud of it too: a man who had never been outside his native country, and never meant to be, if he could help it; that he had been born in Paris, and still thought it the most delightful city in the world; that he had never married, and never intended to marry; and that his lovely wife and three darling children had recently been burned to death in a fire which had also destroyed the ancestral home in Virginia, a tragedy which had so unnerved him that he drank now to forget. This particular tragedy had come at a most inconvenient time, since it occurred on the eve of his defence of his welterweight championship of the world, a title which, since he had not defended it, he had lost by default.

And Lurline, polishing glasses behind her bar, listening patiently to these confused romances of his mind, once shook her head and gave him the only advice she was ever to give him during their association together. 'Charlie! Charlie!' she said reproachfully. 'Never tell a lie that can be *traced*!'

But there was one thing she did know positively about him, aside from the obvious fact that he had money to spend, and spent it freely, and had known from the beginning: he was too weak to manage his life without the help of others, and that fact, rather than his good looks, his youth, his generosity, or the fact that he was said to be 'prominently connected in the East' – a phrase which, for her, had the most fascinating associations – was the thing that attracted her to him; and when he asked her to marry him, and take care of him for ever, after she had taken him to her apartment above the bar and had nursed him through an attack of horrors, she had consented. She was forty-five years old at the time, and he had finished Harvard the year before; but she had not thought the marriage inappropriate at all. She thought it the most natural arrangement in the world for both of them.

She had tried to induce him to cut down on his drinking, but she had not succeeded; then coming to the conclusion that a barroom was not the best place for a man of his temperament, she had had a talk with him one night when he was relatively sober, to discuss his future. Things could not go on this way, she said positively, but in the indulgent accents of the self-sacrificing mother. A time for decision had plainly come. She offered to sell the bar, and go with him to some other place where temptation would not be so strong. She didn't know how he was fixed financially, since he'd told so many conflicting stories regarding the source of his income, but she had a little money put by, and the sale of the bar should keep them going until he was on his feet again, and could take a job. Anyway, she had always been strong, and could turn her hand to almost anything in a pinch. They'd get along, and make a success of their marriage, too; but first he must manage to straighten himself out a bit . . .

He said he had thought of returning to Philadelphia, where he could be near his own family, where they could live in a more conventional atmosphere than was possible on Decatur Street, and where, of course, she could continue to keep an indulgent, supervising eye on him. She had agreed with his plans, had sold her bar, and, leisurely, they had gone to Philadelphia, where they started housekeeping in a handsome brick house which, he explained casually, his godmother had left him some years before.

She had known that he had some income, but she had never thought of his wealth as greater than her own; but at once she saw her mistake, for he was the last of a prolific family whose generative powers had failed in his parents' generation. He had no brothers, no sisters, no immediate cousins – nothing but grandparents, uncles, aunts, and distant connexions, whose individual fortunes he would inherit some day. He was, in a way, the bucket at the bottom of the family tree, the terminal bucket into which all the accumulated sap of the trunk and its auxiliary branches must one day descend.

He had, under his wife's prodding, written to his parents about his marriage, and told them he was bringing his bride home to meet them. He had written so earnestly of her charms, that they had got the impression he had married a famous belle, a young lady of great beauty, and of the most distinguished social position; but when they saw Lurline, they were first shocked into silence, and then, recovering quickly, they made no effort to hide their hostility. Among themselves, they accused her of having tricked their son in order to get his money, which was, perhaps, the only thing they could have said about her that was not true. They had private detectives investigate her career in New Orleans, and when the first reports arrived, they were frantic. They held innumerable family councils, but no matter how greatly they despised Lurline, or deplored their son's impulsive foolishness, the marriage was legal, and there wasn't much they could do about it.

It was at this time that Lurline made her first great error in tactics: she induced her husband to go to a private sanatorium and sober up.

She called on him there a week later, dressed in her best, and looking as implausible in her Victorian finery as those depressed, uneasy policemen, who, to trap a molester of women, put on their wives' clothing and seductively patrol the paths of a park, the handbags at their elbows containing not compacts and powder-puffs, but pistols and saps. She came into the sun-parlour of the sanatorium where, completely sober, in possession of his objective faculties for the first time since she had known him, her husband awaited her. When he looked up and saw her, when he realized who she was, he made a sound of disbelief, backed towards the door, and said, 'Jesus Christ almighty!' One of the young doctors came up, and Charlie, still backing away, said, 'Don't let her touch me!'

It was the first time in years that her feelings had been so badly hurt, and in her confusion she advanced towards him, her face both desperate and coy. 'Why, it's only *Lurline*,' she said. 'I'm not going to hurt you.' But he held on to the doctor's arm and said, 'For God's sake get her out of here!'

She had not attempted to see him again, and when his cure was completed, he went to live with his parents, leaving her alone in the brick house. There, sitting beside her window, staring out at the tree-lined street, she wept and thought scornfully, 'Well, this is a fine thing! – An old strumpet with feelings!' Afterwards, her husband had had a series of love affairs, which she regarded with the completest unconcern; and when the family lawyers, some months afterwards, wrote to her and suggested a divorce, she was entirely agreeable.

At their request, she called at once at their office. They had had none of the difficulties with her which they had been led to expect, and a settlement had been arranged more easily than they had thought possible. Her husband, young Mr Charles Goodpasture, had very few assets, the lawyers explained. His family, as she well knew, were quite wealthy, and although they were prepared to be more generous than the circumstances warranted, perhaps, still they were not of *unlimited* means. They were willing to make a generous adjustment, but they asked a few things in return. First, she must be the guilty party in the divorce, since the Goodpasture reputation must remain unblemished, as a woman of her experience and common sense must surely realize.

'That part's all right,' said Lurline. 'What else?'

In their surprise, the lawyers nodded so sharply that their necks snapped down, and then up, in perfect timing. They went on to say that Mrs Goodpasture must stipulate that she would never see her husband again; that she would make no effort to communicate with him by letter, telegram, telephone, or personal meeting, that she would publish neither a fictional account of their lives together, nor any autobiographical book, sketch, article or other writing, which referred to the Goodpasture family in any manner, favourably or unfavourably, either directly, or by implication.

These latter prohibitions so amused Mrs Goodpasture that she laughed suddenly without disturbing the tightness of her lips or the moroseness of her eyes. She said, 'It's all fine with me. I'm a peasant girl who can't write at all, and who can read nothing but little words in big print.'

The lawyers stared at her soberly, and she went on, 'And here's something else that might surprise the Goodpastures: if I published one-tenth of what I know about Darling Charlie, I'd land in jail before sundown on an obscenity charge.'

'That's splendid,' said the elder of the lawyers. 'You're very cooperative, Mrs Goodpasture, and we're making progress. You're a woman who knows her mind.' Then, feeling perhaps that he had been too cordial, he added cautiously, 'In return for these things, your husband is prepared to give you outright the home and its furnishings where you now reside, excepting the family portraits in oils, or other media, that are now therein; and the Goodpasture family is ready to make you a generous allowance for the term of your natural life.'

Lurline said, 'I don't want a house, and I don't want alimony. I've got my heart set on cash. I want lots of it.'

The lawyers nodded, as if the suggestion both pleased them personally, and simplified matters for their clients. They asked her to name the figure she had in mind, and Lurline, who had not decided on any particular amount, mentioned, as a feeler, the largest sum her mind could comprehend – a hundred thousand dollars.

The lawyers laughed and made deprecatory noises with their

lips, but actually they were pleased, for Mrs Goodpasture had made an error almost as disastrous as the sobering up of her husband had been: she had, as so many of us do, underestimated her repulsiveness to others. She could have doubled her asking price, and have got it as easily, for the Goodpasture family – that association of parents, aunts, uncles, grandparents, and spinster cousins twice removed – was determined to separate Charlie from this battered old harlot who was ruining his life, and their name, no matter what the cost.

The younger of the lawyers said that Lurline must not get the idea the Goodpasture family was *made* of money. There were limits to their generosity. But Lurline got up and said, 'Let me know your decision, gentlemen. The sooner you decide, the sooner we get started.'

There had been no argument at all, and after the divorce had been granted the lawyers wrote her a note informing her that the settlement, in twenty dollar bills as she had stipulated, awaited her. They offered to deposit the money in any bank she named, but Lurline said not to bother, that she'd pick it up herself; and that afternoon she called, with an old telescope-bag under her arm, and collected the rich reward of her bad name.

She never saw her husband again, and had no desire to see him. She went to a cheap hotel for a time, the telescope-bag thrust under the bed. It was here that she received her sister's letter. She met its bearer suspiciously at the door, for she knew at once what he was, and wondered if the Goodpastures, once safely rid of her, had now put the cops on her trail to harass her; but when he explained the purpose of his call she invited him inside and poured him a drink, explaining that she no longer touched it herself, but did keep a bottle for her friends.

She took the letter, examined it, and tossed it contemptuously on the bed; and when the lieutenant asked if she were not anxious to read it, she laughed harshly and said, 'I don't have to read it. She wants money. She's heard I made money on the Goodpasture deal, and now she wants part of it.'

'But you just got the money a couple of weeks ago,' said the lieutenant reasonably, 'and this letter's been floating around for several months. Your sister couldn't have known you'd come into money when she wrote it. That's not possible.'

'That's what you think,' said Lurline. 'Now, let me tell you

something: that one can smell money a thousand miles away.'
Her wit pleased her, and she went on, 'Oh, no, I don't have to
read the letter. I know what's in it. The little sneak wants money.
She wants to grease me up and get it away from me, but she
won't ... Like hell, she'll get it! She'll get it over my dead body
that's how she'll get it!'

Later on, when the lieutenant felt they were on better terms,
had reached a more friendly basis in their relationship, he said,
'The Chief gave me a message for you, Lurline, so I guess it's up
to me to give it: he said he didn't want you opening a place in
Philadelphia.' He finished his drink, wiped his lips on the back
of his hand, and added, 'Well, he told me to tell you that, and I
did so.'

'My God,' said Lurline, 'has the news about me been passed
this far up the line?'

When the lieutenant had departed, four drinks later, Lurline
took up the letter again, but she did not open it. Instead, she
opened the telescope-bag and tossed it in with her settlement, as
though it, too, were a kind of triumph. But the receipt of the
letter, and the visit of the policeman, had alarmed her a little,
had made her feel that she was particularly vulnerable, had
fortified the thought which, for months, had been lying in her
mind: that everybody plotted against her, and envied the little
she had accumulated for herself. She went into a period of
depressed inertia in which she found it difficult to organize her
thoughts, or make plans for her future. In the weeks that followed she seldom left her hotel, feeling that something vague,
but dreadful, would happen to her if she did. She would sit at
her window, looking down at the street and wondering if the
lounger under the lamp at the corner was there by chance, or
had been stationed there to spy on her. She suspected that the
maid discussed her past with the other guests; that the bearded
man across the hall had taken that particular room to rob her;
that the waiter, who served breakfast to her in her room, spilled
coffee in her saucer to show his contempt for her.

When she could stand this strain no longer, she determined to
go back to New Orleans, where the happiest years of her life had
been spent. But she would tell nobody her plans, would reveal to
none her destination; and once there, she would buy a little house
for herself and go into the strictest retirement. She would change

her name; she would see none of her old associates – in fact, she would outwit all those who wished her ill, and had done so for such a long time.

Having reached this decision, the final phase of her disintegrating life began. She closed her bank account; she sold her clothes, her furs, and the jewellery her husband, and others, had given her from time to time; and grasping the telescope-bag in one hand, carrying a suitcase that contained the necessities for her trip in the other, she paid her bill at the desk, walked to the railway station, and bought a ticket to New Orleans.

But she was not destined to reach it, for when she was almost there, the train stopped at a red-brick station beside a wide, yellow river in which water hyacinths were drifting slowly towards the Gulf. Nearby, so close that she could hear the sound of its winches, a steamer was unloading bananas; and, smelling the sweet, heavy scent, she stuck her head out of the coach window and asked the name of the town.

She was told it was Mobile, and she sat back quietly against the rose plush of her seat. Her hands fluttered up twice to her cheeks, and fell again to her lap, where her fingers locked nervously together; then, in a sudden panic she did not understand, and could not have analysed, she seized her two bags and got off the train. She went first to a hotel near the waterfront, to take stock of herself; but when she had formulated her plans in her mind, she walked about the town looking for a place where she could live permanently. The points she considered admirable in the choice of a house were the points others would have considered admirable in the choice of a tomb; but at last she found a place that suited her needs.

It was a small, brick house that was flush with the pavement, with doors and windows that were heavily shuttered. It was dingy, it was dark, it was quiet – and nobody would molest her there. She called at the office of Rushmore & Smart, whose 'For Sale' sign was nailed to the place, and asked to see Mr Rushmore. He took her into his office, and she said, 'My name is Mrs Bessie Pigg. You've got a house for sale that I like. I'm a widow with no children. Now, I might take it. This is my first trip to Mobile. I might take it if it's cheap, that is.'

Mr Rushmore, a jovial man who had never understood that loudness is not necessarily wit, threw back his head and laughed with a sound which was somewhere between the crowing of a rooster and the barking of a dog. 'Mrs Pigg?' he asked ... 'That's a real unusual name.'

'Yes, it is. We were the only Piggs in Toledo.'

'Before we start talking price,' said Mr Rushmore, 'let's get better acquainted. Now, Mrs Pigg, I'm going to ask you a question I ask all my customers, and I hope you'll answer it: what made you pick Mobile to settle in?'

'I like to smell bananas.'

Mr Rushmore's laughter rang out in triumph. He said, 'That's one I never heard before, and I thought I'd heard them all. I must remember to tell my wife that one ... Widow with no children you say?'

'That's right. My husband was an engineer that got scalded to death with steam, as you probably heard.'

'Why, no, I hadn't. That's sad, Mrs Pigg. I guess you miss him. He must have been a fine man.'

'He was a man without a single fault,' said Lurline. 'He didn't smoke, drink, or run after women. In fact, I used to tell him it was too bad, with his name, that he didn't get arrested, at least once, and thrown in jail.'

Mr Rushmore narrowed his eyes in thought. He said, 'I don't get it. I don't see the connexion.'

'If they put him in jail,' said Lurline out of the side of her battered, old-cop's mouth, 'he could always say, "I may not be much, but I'm the only Pigg in *this* pen".'

This time Mr Rushmore turned red from forehead to neck. He almost strangled with laughter, pounding the desk with his open palm. You met all sorts in the real estate business, he knew, but this character was one for the book. He said, when he was able to speak again, 'You know what? – You're a real cute lady, Mrs Pigg!' She made no answer, and he went on, 'Tell me this, ma'am: are you related to the Georgia Piggs?' Then, catching himself up, he shook his head and said in apology, 'But of course you're not related. Their name's *Hogg*.'

'Do they spell it with one g or two g's?' asked Lurline.

'Two g's, ma'am.'

'That's what I thought,' said Lurline. Then petulantly, as though her patience were exhausted with comedians, she added, 'Listen, I pay cash. Do you want to sell the house, or don't you?'

She bought the house and moved in her suitcases that same day. She closed the blinds tightly and sat in the darkened room, looking about her in astonishment, as though wondering how she had got there. She raised her knuckles and rested them against her teeth, thinking, 'Well, what next? What am I waiting for, now?'

Mrs Barnfield was to learn these things in time, but she was not to learn them for some years yet, and concluding that Lurline was lost to her for ever, she dismissed her from her mind. With this old matter settled, with Mate Hansen gone from the island – since she no longer had his visits to look forward to, since she need, now, no longer observe, and record affectionately in her memory, those incidents of the day which she thought might interest him, Irma Barnfield returned to her dedicated search with a passion that embraced all her energies, all her will.

Chapter Ten

IN the months that followed, Mrs Barnfield dug patiently in the hills, she balanced herself on slippery ledges beneath waterfalls, she lowered herself through crevices in the cliffs to investigate the possible existence of caves. Her passion was successful, and in the enthusiastic application of her purpose she found many specimens of the prehistoric writings of October Island, although her main find did not come until the eighth year of her residence there, as we shall see in time.

From the beginning, she had recorded her finds in a notebook, with the date of discovery and a description of each treasure; with a notation of its precise location on the Island when found. She had no doubt but that the Recording Angel of Heaven, who noted and approved her actions, who struck his golden harp and sang a hymn of praise each time she unearthed and destroyed one of her antiquities, was aware of her mounting score as well; but in the press of other activities his record might easily become muddled, his accounting go astray, and she had visions of herself at the day of judgement, standing humbly, but quite firmly, at his elbow, checking, disputing, or, if necessary, amending his errors.

For efficiency, at the end of each season, she digested her discoveries and totalled them on a separate page at the back of her book, as follows:

1895. (Half year only.) One prayer stone.
1896. Fourteen prayer stones. Three chipped. Two badly damaged.
1897. Nine prayer stones, all intact. Forty-two fragments of pottery tablets. One idol of jade, containing no writing, but highly obscene.
1898. No prayer stones. Three clay tablets in good condition. One idol. (Looks like ivory, but not sure.)
1899. Seven prayer stones. Three fragments of tablets. (One quite large.)
1900. One prayer stone. One fragment of clay tablet. (Not much found this year, although worked hard.)

It was at this time, in the beginning of this year that began a new century, that she heard from Mr Hansen for the first time since he had left the Island. When her husband came back from the *Mattie B. Powell*, whose ordinary December trip had been delayed by a typhoon, and handed her the letter, she knew at once whom it was from, although she had never before seen Mr Hansen's writing. She went at once to the summer-house where she would be alone with her thoughts and away from Mr Barnfield's questioning.

The letter was a long one. It contained an itinerary of his travels since she had seen him last, and it alluded to, but did not amplify, 'the many interesting and instructive experiences' he'd recently had. He had meant to write long before this, but somehow he hadn't, being lazy and inclined to put things off as she well knew. He hoped her health was excellent as usual and that the Reverend Barnfield, who had not been feeling too well the last time he saw him, was now entirely recovered. He had given up the sea, for the time being at any rate; and while this would surprise her, while she might not approve the new direction his life had taken, he was in vaudeville at present and doing quite well there, too.

She looked up for an instant and, as if personally addressing the nutmeg tree that grew nearby, she said aloud, 'Merciful heavens, what does he think I am – some narrow-minded old fogy? ... Mr Barnfield might think such conduct sinful, but certainly I do not.'

She turned a page to discover that he was now playing Chicago.

His new career had come about by chance. Here were the facts: while in 'Frisco, between ships, he had met a young lady who was an entertainer, a dancer to be precise. Her name was Miss Carmen Dilustro. She was a vivacious girl with a wonderful sense of humour and she had been on the stage since childhood. Well, to make a long story short, he and some of his shipmates had dropped into the café where Miss Dilustro was dancing, and in the interval between performances, the boys had asked him to sing some of the Hawaiian songs he used to sing for them on shipboard. They'd made such a point of the matter he couldn't very well refuse, and when one of the members of the orchestra laughed and handed him a steel guitar, he had done the best he could.

Miss Dilustro, who had dark, sparkling eyes of remarkable brilliance, had been sitting at a table on the balcony with friends. She had been impressed by his voice and had arranged a meeting with him after her next performance. Hawaii had just been made

106

a part of the United States, as Mrs Barnfield of course knew, and Queen Liliuokalani's visit to America had been widely publicized. Since these things were true, Miss Dilustro had seen no reason why Hawaiian music should not become popular, and as a novelty singing-and-dancing act she suggested they team up and call themselves The Blond Hawaiians.

Miss Dilustro, despite her sweetness and tolerance for all, was an intelligent girl with no foolishness about her. It was impossible not to admire her.

At first he had thought the idea impractical, but later on he had come to see the possibilities in it. Miss Dilustro was of Sicilian descent and almost as dark as himself, which she considered an asset for their act. Her hair was dark, too, but she had bleached it yellow to match his own. They were doing well together, although things were a bit off at the moment and engagements not so plentiful as they would be later on in the season. Miss Dilustro was truly a lovely girl and he had grown quite fond of her in the six months they had been together.

'My gracious!' said Mrs Barnfield. 'I wonder what he wears in front of all those people?'

She glanced back at the letter and found her answer at once. He wore silk trunks beneath a tasselled skirt such as the October Islanders wore, but this time the skirt was not made of finely shredded palm fibres, but of silver undulating silk. There was a longer description of Miss Dilustro's costume, but as this did not interest her in the slightest Mrs Barnfield skimmed through it in boredom.

The act opened with him playing his guitar and singing a love song against a backdrop of water and palm trees, while Miss Dilustro did her hula dance. Later, he sang again, and the act closed with a dance together, a dance which was supposed to be Hawaiian but which had never been seen there, or anywhere else, so far as he knew.

Miss Dilustro, in addition to being so talented and beautiful, was a kindly person of domestic tastes. It was most pleasant to be associated with her professionally. She was teaching him many things.

At this point Mrs Barnfield put down the letter and said in exasperation, 'All right! All right! You don't have to drop a ton of bricks on me!' Then, speaking petulantly to the nutmeg tree,

107

she added, 'If she's all that wonderful, why isn't her picture in magazines, and why hasn't everybody heard of her before this? What was a remarkable girl like that doing dancing in a water-front café in San Francisco, I'd like to know!'

But almost at once she was ashamed of her jealousy, and, having ventilated it, she sighed, touched her eyes with her hand-kerchief, and told the nutmeg tree that most certainly she had no desire to defeat Mr Hansen's happiness. She was glad he'd found such a fine girl to love, and she'd be quite content for them to marry soon and settle down. Mr Hansen was a perfectly wonder-ful young man with many long years before him. He deserved the best that life had to offer, and she was prepared to give his bride the same unselfish affection that she gave him ...

But she could not sustain the mood, could not delude herself for long, for she knew in her heart that she meant none of the admirable sentiments she had forced her lips to utter, and saying, 'Oh, fiddlesticks!' to herself, she determined to write him a long letter in return, a letter in which she would deal with the intruding Miss Dilustro by ignoring her entirely. But when she examined the letter and envelope she saw that he had given no address at all – he had not even mentioned by name the theatre where he was playing.

She looked up, tapping the letter against her thumb, and saw that her husband approached the summer-house. She had not seen him closely for a long time, not for the five years of her im-passioned search, but now, regarding him with the same objecti-vity with which the Islanders must habitually regard him, she was surprised at the manner in which he had aged. He walked with little, mincing steps these days, putting down each foot as though it were precious to him, for this continent, saintly old man who neither drank, smoked, nor indulged in rich foods suffered the punishments that are promised the drun-kard, the glutton, and the lecher as an atonement for their pleasures.

He had an enlarged liver, but he had known that for a long time, and in a sense he had come to accept his affliction as average and to be expected; but of late, he had also been plagued by days of dull, almost unbearable, prostatic pain. He suffered such pain at this moment as he approached his wife where she sat in the summer-house and lowered himself carefully to the seat beside her, frowning a little as though it were difficult to concentrate on anything outside his own misery.

In answer to his question Mrs Barnfield said casually, 'The letter was from Mr Hansen. He's quite well, and wrote from Chicago. He asked to be remembered to you, and expressed a wish that your health is much improved.'

In the days that followed she read the letter over and over, wondering what subtlety of meaning, meant for her eyes alone, lay hidden behind each seemingly innocent phrase. She thought of Mate Hansen a great deal at that period, remembering the stimulating conversations they had had together, the many little courtesies he had shown her as tokens of his regard; and then, becoming restless at all this interest in the past, a past which she certainly had no power to recall, even if she wanted to, she turned to the realities of her search once more.

The year 1901 proved an excellent one for her, despite the fact that some of her time that year was taken up with other matters. In it, she found six prayer stones (all perfect), seven clay tablets (one chipped, one with small, diagonal split), and two idols (in prime condition) – one of Rahabaat, one of his consort. All these treasures she washed, examined dutifully, and threw into the volcano.

She began, at that time, to explore the far side of the island, which before she had neglected: at a place where, in the remote past when Min-Rahabaat had been an active volcano, the lava from its eruptions had scored the sides of the hills as it flowed to the sea, to be extinguished there. She examined this area without success, but not really expecting to find anything in so wild and unpromising a place, and one morning, being tired from her labours and exhausted by the heat, she returned to the grove of palms where she had left the instruments of her profession.

She concluded that this spot was as good as any to eat her lunch in, but when she looked for her box she could not find it. The loss annoyed her for she was hungry and it was a long way back to her cottage; and she retraced her steps, searching the underbrush to discover, if she could, where the lunch box had fallen. She did not find it, but farther along, on the side of one of the small, rolling hills, she came upon one of those altars on which the natives set food for Rahabaat, should that divinity, in passing by, feel the need for refreshment. There was fruit, coconut milk, smoked fish, and several objects wrapped in banana leaves, all lying devoutly on the stone. She opened the first of these leafy parcels: it was roast young pig, so freshly cooked, so recently placed on the altar, that it was still warm.

The aroma of the roast pig, which she had released when she opened the leaves, was too tantalizing to be endured, and for a moment she stood in indecision, wondering if, by taking the food, she would be stealing; but after a little thought she saw the senselessness of such a strict application of morals: the food had been given to Rahabaat, so it no longer belonged to its original owner; and since Rahabaat existed only in the childish minds of those who believed in him, it could not belong to him either. It was plainly in the public domain, like an old book whose copyright had lapsed. 'Oh, dear,' she said. 'It seems a pity to waste this nice food when I'm almost starved. Really, I don't see the slightest harm in taking it.'

Having made up her mind she selected a red, sugary fig from the shell where it rested and ate it in two dainty bites. 'Delicious!' she said. 'Absolutely *delicious!*' She seated herself on one corner of the altar and lunched picnic-fashion. She had just bitten into the roast pork when, hearing a peculiar sound in the underbrush, she turned and met the startled eyes of one of the fishermen who lived in this part of the island. His opened mouth, the stunned expression in his eyes, amused her, and she laughed self-consciously, and said in a voice which was somewhat too loud, somewhat too defensive, 'It isn't stealing, really. If I didn't eat it, then the birds would.'

The fisherman remained silent. He continued to stare at her with his shocked eyes, and Mrs Barnfield, becoming nervous under his disapproving gaze, laughed shrilly, held out a banana to him, and said, 'Won't you join me?' She got up from the altar and walked towards the transfixed man. 'Don't be silly!' she said. 'Eat it! It won't hurt you in the slightest, I assure you!'

At that the fisherman found the power to move again, and making a strangled noise in his throat, moving his arms rapidly from side to side in a gesture to ward off evil, he backed away to a safe distance; then, turning abruptly, he ran as fast as he could down the hill. He went first to his own village, to tell the unbelievable things he had seen, and the people listened to him in wonderment; but not knowing how to handle such an

110

unprecedented situation, they went in a body to the kampong of the Radja to put the matter before him.

In turn the Radja called in the High Priest, his three advisers, and Brenan-Oan. 'I don't see that it's anything to concern ourselves about,' said the Radja in a cross, petulant, voice. 'The woman is dead by this time and the matter is thus solved. Nobody eats the food of Rahabaat and lives: at least, no mortal does. That is a fact known to all, and has been known since time began.'

'But is this Mrs Barnfield mortal?' asked Brenan-Oan. 'She is like nothing ever seen on this island.'

'She is most strange,' said the Radja, in fairness. 'She is engaged on a mission that baffles us all; but whatever that mission is it is designed to benefit ourselves and not her, for she returns all her discoveries to Rahabaat, the true owner of everything. Who knows the motives behind her actions? Perhaps Rahabaat instructs her in dreams and she, with her seeking and digging, fulfils his desires.'

'She is married and yet she is untouched,' said the High Priest. 'That is a most strange thing, as all admit.'

'She listens to nothing her husband says, as a married woman should,' said Brenan-Oan. 'Her husband stands in awe of her as we stand in awe of our goddess Kallapaaga. He fears to correct the oddities of her behaviour, as any husband would correct the oddities of a mortal wife.'

'Perhaps he is not her husband,' said the Radja. 'Perhaps he is one whose spirit she has snared, whom she has enchanted to do her bidding and abide near her for appearance' sake, since a virgin cannot, with propriety, travel the world alone.'

'Her dress is odd,' said the High Priest. 'Her speech is odd. Her temperament is the oddest of all. She is a peculiar woman.'

'At least she is a magician, as we all know,' said Brenan-Oan. 'When Toppateeter was ill she brought her a charm of great magic power, and put it about her neck to ward off evil. It was a talisman of the very highest holiness. She confided these facts to Toppateeter, who was her friend, and Toppateeter, in turn, told others before she died.'

'But her charm was not at all useful,' said the High Priest. 'It could not make the crab desist from his task.'

111

'The crab is powerful,' said the Radja shortly. 'Even the thighbone of Kaplinja is powerless against him.'

They discussed Mrs Barnfield for a long time, and then they decided to go to the hills and see what had happened to her. They paused when they heard the rhythmic sound of activity before them, and pulling back the underbrush they saw that Mrs Barnfield had not died at all. Instead, refreshed by her meal, she was swinging her pick with renewed vigour, grunting happily in the afternoon sun. She saw them peering at her and thought, 'It's about eating that silly food, I suppose. I hope they're not going to be *tiresome!*'

She had been guilty of an indiscretion, she felt, although a perfectly natural one; but she had no wish to offend the natives of this place where she must live and where she was so happy; and knowing how jealously they guarded the tenets of their faith she suddenly had an inspired thought: she would save both her face and their own by pretending she did not know the purpose of the food on the altar, that she had assumed it was placed there for herself as an act of courtesy; and having come to this conclusion she wiped her brow and said, 'I must thank you for the lunch. It was delicious, and it was most thoughtful of you to leave it for me ... But how could you have known I'd lost my lunch box?'

The delegation looked at one another significantly, but they did not speak; and after staring back at them for a time Mrs Barnfield said, 'You must excuse me now. I'm quite busy, as you see,' and went on with her work. But on that particular day she found nothing to reward her, and when the sun was between the cones of Min-Rahabaat she went towards her home.

As she approached one of the mountain streams she heard her husband's voice raised in a fervent scolding. He was, she saw quickly, preaching to a group of sago makers who, since they could not escape, worked in silence, trying to give the preacher's words that polite consideration which they felt all words deserved. He was delivering his sermon on the durian tree, one of his favourites which she had heard many times, and as she paused unseen she heard him say:

'When I offer you sternness, deprivation, and austerity of the flesh, perhaps you think these things are not attractive, in view of your own philosophy of eternal joy and unrestrained pleasure.

112

'Now, each of you, as a man of experience and common sense, is familiar with the fruit of the durian tree. You must know, having seen it all your lives, how repellent it is with its strong, disagreeable odour. At first it seems unattractive, unappetizing, and not worth while when compared with the commonplace flavours of the orange, the banana, and the coconut – those ordinary fruits that all admire.

'It requires courage to taste of the durian fruit, but once a man has done so he renounces the insipidities of lesser fruits, for the durian is so satisfying when tasted, so nourishing, so fulfilling of all man's secret needs, that he will never again be content with lesser fruit.

'So it is with the doctrines of the Gospel Prophets. At first the harshness, the discipline, and the deprivations that I offer you may seem repellent in your eyes; but once the fruit of the tree is in your mouths, then you will be filled with nourishment for ever; then you will renounce your evil lives of lust and indolence for the sterner joys of salvation; then you will – '

All at once Mrs Barnfield had a sense of irritation at her husband. In the past she had admired his sermons and had listened to them with a most flattering attention, regarding them as works of art and wondering where, in his unremarkable mind, he found the imagery with which to adorn the simplest phrases of everyday life; but now she drew back farther among the trees, thinking the sago makers were quite right in snubbing him. 'Mr Barnfield is a silly man in many ways,' she said to herself. 'It's strange, but I never realized it before.' She felt ashamed of him, and she neither wanted to acknowledge him before others, nor to pay him the compliment of listening to the triteness of his sermon; but she, like the sago makers, was trapped for the time being, and she waited beside the tree in patience. When he had finished his sermon and had asked the sago makers to openly embrace the doctrines of The Gospel Prophets, an invitation which they refused with giggles, shakes of their heads, and embarrassed side glances at one another, the Reverend Barnfield sighed, turned away, and walked off with his precise, cautious steps; but Mrs Barnfield, when he had gone a safe distance, took another way home, and when he arrived at his cottage she was already there, preparing his supper.

Later that afternoon the Radja and his advisers sat in conference a long time. They came at last to a most important decision: Mrs Barnfield was plainly of divine origin, but whether related by blood or loyalty to their own gods, they did not as yet know. She was obviously a being too powerful to be thwarted or hindered. They would watch her. They would humour her wishes. They would treat her with deference. She would reveal herself, and her purpose, in time, if that suited her wish. They would wait and see.

After that, Mrs Barnfield did not bother to carry lunch at all, for no matter where she happened to be on the island when she stopped her work at noon and seated herself to rest, there was always fresh food for her needs, delivered so quietly, so deftly, that often she wondered how it got there. As she walked about the island, the natives, who met her on a path or near the lagoon or approaching the village of the Radja, would pause and stand with bowed, submissive heads, their arms extended towards her, their wrists crossed in a gesture of their servitude. If she spoke to them they would listen, their lips silently shaping the words she uttered, as though thus to impress her wisdom on their minds for ever; when she had finished they would quietly vanish.

She did not know what had happened, what had changed her status so dramatically, and she did not care too much. She went about her appointed work, digging, seeking, finding, and discarding: knowing in her accomplishment a feeling of peace, a sense of her own importance which she had never before experienced.

In the late summer of 1901 the Reverend Barnfield came down with an illness that lasted a long time. He complained of severe pains in his back and thighs, and his chest was so sensitive that he could not bear to have it touched. His eyes ached and his head burned, and at night he often tossed about and cried out in delirium. Mrs Barnfield was greatly concerned about him, and in the weeks that followed she gave up her search to take care of him, to be constantly at his side. She hoped that he'd soon recover, but he did not, and at last she became greatly alarmed. She wished there were some way to take him to Honolulu, but since the *Mattie B. Powell* would not return until December, and there was no other communication between October Island and the outside world, there was nothing she could do but pray and give him home remedies.

He showed no improvement at all, and when his suffering was so great she could no longer endure it, she remembered the deadening drink that the *brunga-brungas* prepared for their patients. But she knew Mr Barnfield, no matter how great his pain, would never voluntarily take the remedies a heathen medicine-man prepared, and so she went one morning to discuss the problem with Brenan-Oan, feeling that her position on the Island was now too important to permit her dealing with the *brunga-brungas* in person. There was no point in hurting the feeling of the Islanders, who were most sensitive, as she had already discovered, so she told him of her husband's condition, and added that while the medicine of the *brunga-brungas* would not ordinarily have effect on a foreigner like himself, it could, by the addition of magic remedies of her own, be modified and made to serve its purpose. She wondered if he could get her a supply of the medicine that killed pain, and he said he would do so at once.

He brought her the opiate an hour later, with full instructions as to dosage in this particular emergency. He said, too, that the *brunga-brungas*, while they had not been called in professionally, had been aware of the Reverend Barnfield's interesting condition for a long time, and had often discussed it among themselves. They all agreed that he was suffering from old-man-complaint, and since they were sure of their diagnosis, they had taken the liberty of preparing a medicine for him. It was compounded from a formula which had been passed down for thousands of years – a prescription whose ingredients they alone knew.

If the Reverend Barnfield objected to taking the medicine, Mrs Barnfield, after adding her own remedies, could administer it to him in broth, or strong tea, and he'd never know the difference. She did what the *brunga-brungas* advised and her husband's pain stopped almost at once; then, to his surprise, but not her own, he began slowly to mend, to take an interest in the world about him once more.

When he was out of danger and able to walk about the house, with a cane to support his trembling legs, she had one of the local carpenters make a rattan couch for him to lie on, and she put him out on the terrace, beneath the young grey-and-green striped palm that he admired so much, where he could be alone with his thoughts, and show his face, which still had a trace of

115

death on it, to the blue, glittering sea; and as he lay so quietly, as though already dead, in the soft sunlight, he contemplated eternity, trying to measure it with thought . . .

Once, when he was younger, he had wished for a preview of paradise, some prevision through trance or dream of the glory that awaited in heaven, as many before him had had in their lifetime; but the ecstasy had been denied him, and now he was glad, for as he lay so passively beneath the palm tree, he pictured his first, naïve rapture when, like an uninstructed child, he viewed God in fresh innocence, while His choirs of angels sang psalms of joy and his golden throne and jewelled streets glistened in light, as the sea did at this moment. He would spend long hours thus, nodding, remembering, sleeping, and waking once more to reality. He made up a poem from the names of the palm trees he remembered, and often he would recite it to himself:

> *Palmyra, areca, borassus, arenga,*
> *And the coconut palm.*
>
> *Lontar, gebanga, rattan, and nipa,*
> *And the gingerbread palm.*
>
> *Talipot, buri, makapuno, and sago,*
> *And the sweet sugar palm.*
>
> *Zalacca, pinanga, licuala, corypha,*
> *And the sealing-wax palm.*
>
> *Salak, pigafettia, orania palindan,*
> *Livistona, kavesu, and date,*
> *And the great royal palm.*
>
> *And the coconut palm,*
> *And the gingerbread palm.*
> *And the sweet sugar palm.*
> *And the sealing-wax palm.*
> *And the great royal palm . . .*
>
> *And the great royal palm.*

When he had finished his poem, his eyes would fill with tears for reasons he never understood; but he would brush them away, smile, turn on his side, and sleep again.

Chapter Eleven

IN April of 1902, the October Islanders began preparations for the observance of *Faraal Marzaan*. Mrs Barnfield felt the excitement everywhere, and in order to post herself on the festival's history and meaning, she went once more to the encyclopedias the anthropologists had left behind in her cottage. She learned that the festival was observed once every ten years, which was, in the belief of the Islanders, the length of time that Raha had pursued Baat through the skies, and beneath the seas, before their union was consummated on the spot where October Island now existed.

There were nine preliminary days of feasting, ceremonies, and games, with maskers and dancers everywhere, like some pagan Mardi Gras; but these preparatory days were only an interlude of pleasure, a preparation for the great tenth day, the mystic day of Baat's capture.

The rites on this final day began at sunrise with a symbolic fertilization of the lontar palms, and since this observance was not considered secret it had been witnessed by several of the Island's visitors, among them Muriel Hawkins and Dr Clement Higgs. It was thought likely, although not definitely determined, that the remainder of the day was devoted to prayer, fasting, the chanting of songs which recited the glories of Shurabast, and to performance in secret of those ancient fertility dances which the priests and their concubines had once staged in the great temple. The religious aspects of the festival ended at sunset, in a ceremony so sacred that no native could be induced to describe it; later there was a feast and dancing at a place whose location was not known, although Muriel Hawkins was of the opinion that it occurred somewhere on the south end of the island, near the eroded cliffs.

The Reverend Barnfield was anxious to see the commencing ceremony on the tenth day, and, still a little weak from his illness, still leaning on his cane for support, he arose while it was dark and went to the grove of lontar palms near the harbour where this initiatory rite would take place. He had asked his wife if she cared to go with him, but she had shaken her head disdainfully and said she had better things to occupy her attention.

It was still dark when he reached the palms, but already a great group of the Islanders had gathered there before him. They stood assembled in silence, their eyes lifted earnestly to the east, to witness the first sight of Raha as he appeared above the horizon. To the left, beneath a canopy of palm leaves, were the Radja, his advisers, the High Priest, Brenan-Oan, and the ten boys and ten girls who had been selected to take part in the ceremony.

He grew restless with waiting, wondering if the sun would rise at all that day. He closed his eyes for an instant, and when he opened them again the tip of the sun was visible above the sea. At that moment the chorus began its hymn of praise, and the Radja turned and offered the High Priest the long flower cluster of the male palm. The priest blessed the male cluster, and with his lips moving in prayer he tore from its stem the little pollen-covered buds. When this was done the plume of the female palm was brought to him, and he blessed it too, and prepared it for fertilization. It was at this instant, before Raha had freed himself from the rim of the sea, that the ten naked boys and the ten naked girls began their slow, circular dance around the High Priest and sang to the accompaniment of the musicians:

> *Praised be thy fertility, Rahabàat!*
> *May it remain strong for us;*
> *May it never fail its purpose.*
>
> *May the desire of the one for the other never fail,*
> *That the earth may endure for ever.*
>
> *That the trees, and the plants, and the grasses*
> *And all other things endure for ever.*
>
> *Cursed be the one that denies his flesh,*
> *Or hides from it in the cavern of his windy mind.*
> *May his courage fail.*
>
> *May his hand fail.*
> *May his sight fail.*
> *May his heart flutter and fail.*
>
> *May he drink bitterness.*
> *May he dine alone,*
> *The one that denies flesh.*
> *May he be forgotten.*

Later, when Raha was not high above the rim of the sea, the boys and girls received the flower clusters from the High Priest, and holding them above their heads they ran with them towards the interior of the island, while the people fell in behind them in a singing and shouting procession. Then, when the crowd had dispersed, Sam Barnfield went home slowly, pausing to rest along the way.

His wife was fixing breakfast when he arrived, and he saw immediately that she was in a state of excitement. A most unusual thing had happened, she said: the High Priest and Brenan-Oan had just called on her and had invited her to preside over the evening ceremonials which would close the festival. If she would so honour the Islanders, a chair would be sent for her, and she would be taken to the place of celebration in comfort.

'Naturally you're not going,' said Sam. 'You thanked them, and told them No, of course.'

'Certainly I'm going,' said Irma. 'It's an honour to be asked. I just read in the encyclopedias that no outsider ever saw one of these ceremonies: not even the anthropologists, who tried so hard, could manage to get in.'

'That's a strange attitude to take, Mrs Barnfield.'

'It's nothing but a masquerade party, when you come right down to it,' she said impatiently ... 'Now, please quit pestering me, because I've got to think up something to wear. I can't go in my regular clothes. That would be out of the question.'

The Reverend Barnfield said sternly, 'Madam, are you aware of the fact that your religion forbids feasting, dancing, and levity of conduct?'

'I'm as aware of that fact as you are, Mr Barnfield ... Now, kindly go on about your business, and leave me alone.'

'Are you also aware that your beliefs prohibit the wearing of dress designed to entice or allure the mind?'

'I know these things quite well, I assure you. I should know them by this time: I've been hearing them all my life.'

'Have you no shame left, Mrs Barnfield? Have you lost all sense of decency?'

'If you'll mind your business, and let me handle mine, I'll consider it a favour, Mr Barnfield.'

'What would your father say if he could see you in some

heathen costume at a pagan ball? ... I know quite well what he'd say, and so do you.'

'Papa's opinion isn't of the slightest interest to me, I assure you,' said Mrs Barnfield. She smoothed her hair and explained that all her life she had been taking orders from others, on the assumption that their judgement was better than her own; but she was through with all that foolishness. From now on, she was doing as she pleased, responsible only to her own conscience, and completely unconcerned with the opinions of others, who seemed to think they knew so much.

The Reverend Barnfield stared at her as though she were suddenly demented, and she went on to say that she realized at last what her basic problem had always been: she had lacked confidence in herself! ... Everybody had belittled her, all her life. They had tried to convince her she was an evil person of no importance. She had accepted these views with meekness, and without examination, which, when she looked back now, she thought was rather silly of her. She reminded her husband of the esteem the October Islanders had for her, and how they treated her as a woman of significance and power. Being invited to this great, final ceremony of *Faraal Marzaan* was proof enough of her contentions, and until he himself had achieved a similar position of love and trust among the Islanders, she suggested that he keep his big, Vermont mouth shut, and not go around criticizing those who had.

She moved away from him, shrugging her shoulders, but paused, and turned slowly, when he said: 'I forbid it! I will not permit you to attend this pagan spectacle!'

She was so overcome with amusement that she leaned against the door sill for support. Then, slowly, a sense of anger came over her, and again she lost her temper with her husband, although she'd promised herself she'd never do so again. She strode over to him, slapped the table with her open palm, and said, '*You* forbid it? Who do you think you are? You've got a lot to learn, I must say!'

She spoke shrilly, her voice tight and furious, and slapping rhymically on the table for emphasis, she wondered if he knew what the natives called him behind his back? Well, if he didn't, she'd be glad to enlighten him: They called him *Nupoona dool Palladole*, and if he didn't know what that meant in English, it meant 'Old dried-up talking-bone!' They laughed at him, and made jokes about the sermons he thought so wonderfully inspiring. When they saw him coming, they ran away, as though escaping the plague ... And, in a way, she didn't blame them: what did he have to offer them that they didn't *already* have? She talked on and on, saying all the things she should have said to Papa years ago, her voice getting louder and louder.

When she had finished, Sam said, 'You have changed a great deal. I hardly recognize you any more.'

'Thank you very much,' said Irma bitingly. She moved away in the direction of the terrace, adding over her shoulder, 'That's the nicest compliment anybody ever paid me.'

'Mrs Barnfield,' said her husband sadly, 'you're a lost woman.'

She stopped on the veranda, stuck her head through the door, and said, 'And you, Reverend Barnfield, are a dirty-minded old man.'

She walked for a time on the terrace, until her anger had subsided, and her hands were no longer trembling; then she went to the store-room, wondering what costume she should wear that evening. Her dress, she felt, should be in keeping with the traditions of the festival; and after a little thought she made her decision: she would go as the Evening Star. There was a bolt of cheesecloth on the shelves; there were the Christmas tree ornaments which they had carried with them about the world; there was enough cardboard; there was silver and gilt paint; she would manage very well indeed!

She went to work at once, and that night, when the moon rose, as the chair and its bearers arrived, she was ready in a robe cut along Grecian lines, with train and full, flowing sleeves. Around her throat was a necklace of small, gilded stars, which she had cut from pasteboard and had strung together with thread; at her waist there was a silver girdle of larger stars, knotted loosely like a schoolgirl's sash. Gilded stars were sewn to the hem of her skirt, and below them her silvered sandals advanced and disappeared as she walked across her veranda and down the steps. A gilded cardboard crown encircled her skull, a crown from which a tall column rose. At the top of the column there was affixed, in turn, a glittering, silver star which had once adorned the tip of a Christmas tree. She had loosened her hair, and it rippled and hung almost to her ankles; and as the bearers advanced and lifted her into the chair, they gaped at her magnificence.

They carried her rapidly in the direction of Min-Rahabaat, and Mrs Barnfield, looking into the moonlit darkness about her, thought with satisfaction, 'Miss Muriel Hawkins isn't as smart as she *thinks* she is: the celebration isn't held anywhere near the cliffs; in fact, we're going in the opposite direction ... My guess is that it's held on that big plateau between the cones.'

Later on, when the bearers reached the site of the old temple, they turned off into a valley, and pausing before a mass of shrubs they entered a shallow cave in the side of one of the hills. They came out presently on to a flat, grassy place – and there the assembled people were waiting. At Mrs Barnfield's approach they lowered their heads and extended their crossed arms towards her; but she called out gaily, 'Please! Please! Don't let me interrupt the festivities. Go on with what you were doing!'

The drinking and eating had not as yet begun, but beyond her, in the grove, the great feast was being prepared, the aroma of roasting fowl, fish, and young, tender pig, coming strongly to her nostrils; soon, now, the wine cups would be passing from hand to hand; soon, now, the celebrants would perhaps be engaging in those orgies of which she had heard so much from other, more worldly, missionaries. She turned her eyes a little and saw the dancers gathered at the edge of the trees, waiting their cues to perform; and as she sat there so straight-backed and gracious in her chair, her stars and draperies swirling about her, she wondered if her husband had not been correct in his advice to her; if, after all, her patronage at this celebration were not a mistake ...

They assisted her to the throne that had been fixed for her, but before seating herself on it she turned slowly so that all might see her, and said, 'I represent Venus, the Evening Star. I hope you like my costume.'

There was a shout of approval from the people, for at last their visitor had confessed her identity to them: she was *Mona-Varaal*, the loveliest of all Baat's tears, the great, brilliant star who shone both in the morning and in the evening.

Mrs Barnfield acknowledged the applause, and, standing with her hair rippling softly between her crown and stars, she affirmed her allegiance to October Island and her love for its people. She considered the invitation an honour, she said – one which she would always remember and appreciate; then, glancing once more at the dancers and thinking it wise to leave an opening for herself, an opening which would save both her own face and the faces of her hosts if things became too impossible later on, she added, 'I'd like to remain with you until the end of the feast, but perhaps that will not be possible for reasons I cannot go into ... But if it is necessary for me to leave early, I hope you will understand that I have many things to occupy my attention these days.'

When she had finished her speech, the Radja, the High Priest and Brenan-Oan, approached and knelt before her. They were all masked, but she felt she would have recognized Brenan-Oan anywhere! He had, she thought, the finest pair of legs on the Island, now that Mr Hansen was no longer there. Perhaps, in a way, his legs were even *better* than Mr Hansen's ... It was true they were neither so straight, so muscular, nor so nicely coloured, but they were certainly more symmetrical at the calf, and perhaps even better turned at ankle and knee. It was all a matter of taste, really! ... Then, as she smiled and acknowledged the homage being paid her, she thought ruefully, 'Shapely young men are my weakness. There's no point in trying to delude myself on that point any longer.'

Later on, after the assistant priests, the *brunga-brungas* and the Radja's advisers had made the obeisances due to a goddess, Brenan-Oan returned with a long box wrapped in a towel of blue feathers, and she thought patiently, 'Here comes Kaplinja's mouldy thighbone again. It looks as though you can't escape it on this island.' But she concealed her boredom, and Brenan-Oan exhibited the treasure to her. She did not know what was expected of her, but she examined the relic thoughtfully; then, when she had finished her inspection, and it was in its case and wrapped once more, she asked, as though to lend a touch of realism to her performance, to see it again. This time she concentrated her gaze on the knobby tip of the bone, as though verifying some basic fact which she had suspected from the first, and saying 'Ah-h-h!' in a loud, pleased voice, she returned the bone to its keeper.

When these preliminary courtesies had been carried out, the Radja asked if she were now ready for the ceremonies to begin, and when she nodded and said she was, he gave the necessary commands. Later, when she was home again, she complimented herself on her foresight in laying the groundwork for her sudden

123

but dignified exit, for some of the things she had seen that night had not been in good taste; and as she turned gently on her mattress, so as not to wake her husband, she wondered if she was as broadminded as she thought. It was a difficult thing to determine, she felt – like all generalities; and resting her cheek on one palm, she sighed and said under her breath, 'Well, anyway, I'm broadminded for a *missionary*.'

The ceremonies had begun with a three-part dance called 'The Creation of October Island'. The first movement, danced by a selected group of men, was sub-titled 'The Silliness of Women'. For the occasion each man wore a mask with crossed eyes, broken nose, and wide, crooked mouth; each wore, as well, a wig of shredded palm fibres to represent the long, coarse hair of the women. Each wore the women's skirt, and about the shoulders of each, fixed to a heavy, leather harness, were two plump, elongated gourds painted a bright blue.

When the introductory music was finished the men moved to the grassy arena with little steps of delicate elegance, fingering their long hair, fluffing it out at the sides and chattering shrilly of their charms. They stamped their feet and pretended to quarrel among themselves; but, adjusting their differences somehow, they moved together to the edge of the ring, the right arm of each dancer resting on the shoulder of his neighbour, and with their blue gourds swaying hypnotically they undulated their hips from side to side and up and down in the stylized rhythm prescribed for them. The dance went on for a long time, the movements becoming progressively more difficult, more involved; but when at last it was finished, and when all phases of the silliness of women had been explored, the men retired to the back of the arena, one arm resting in provocation on their hips, the other holding their gourds outward, and offering them to all alike.

At this point Mrs Barnfield fanned herself and moved restively on her throne, a strained look in her eyes. She half rose from her seat and then, settling back once more, she thought, 'I'll stay for the second part. Maybe it won't be as bad as the first.'

The second movement of the dance was called 'The Arrogance of Men', and the women who had been waiting their turn to perform it, came striding on to the grassy place, as realistically equipped for their roles as the men had been for theirs. It was at this point that Mrs Barnfield had known how the dance would

124

end: both men and women would take part in the final movement – with no costumes on at all, probably! It would be bad enough to see October Island created *once*, she thought ... But to see it created *ten times*, simultaneously, before her eyes –

'Well!' said Mrs Barnfield. '*Well*, now!'

She decided she'd better go home at once, while she had the opportunity, and after the women had completely established the arrogance of men, she stood up and asked for her bearers. At once her chair was brought to her, and she stepped into it, nodding gravely to all, and was taken to her own door. The Radja, the High Priest, Brenan-Oan, and even the lesser people themselves, were pleased at her tact and discernment, and as she disappeared through the entrance to the cave they nodded their heads in approval, as though to say that only a goddess of the stature of The Evening Star herself knew precisely how long to remain at a party.

When the celebration was over and October Island was its normal self again, Mrs Barnfield resumed her search, but with indifferent results. One afternoon she decided to dispose of the one prayer stone (eroded; badly chipped), and the one clay tablet (writing obliterated), which she had recently uncovered, and without waiting to find others, she set out on her journey up the sides of Min-Rahabaat. The trip was a tiring one, and when her task was completed she seated herself on a stone, leaned back against another, and surveyed the surrounding scene with the proprietor's eye that she had long had for this place.

The Island lay minified and remote beneath her, with the tops of its trees stretching outward in a dense mass of contrasted green: an uneven carpet which ran from this green place where she rested to the more delicate green of the shallow water at the shore. A crowd of boys and girls were swimming in the lagoon, and even at this distance, as she yawned sleepily and shook her head, she could hear the occasional high, excited sound of their voices – not as individual words with meaning, but as pure tone in the shrill crystal of the air.

She nodded and closed her eyes for what she thought was only an instant; and then, as if aware somehow, even through her sheltering lids, that the picture about her had darkened, she sat up straight and saw that a long, fish-like cloud had floated in from the east and was now advancing languidly beneath her, between the great cones of the volcano itself. She saw how, beyond the fat, fig-coloured cloud, the rays of the sun vibrated and glittered on the tree tops, the light dying abruptly away as the cloud moved forward and encompassed the landscape; then as she watched, so detached, so remote from what was happening in the tiny world below her, the cloud opened in a drenching downpour of rain ...

In the villages she could see the sudden activity, with fibre windows being closed as the people laughed and warned one another of the cloudburst; then, slowly the cloud returned to the sea and October Island was its familiar self again, with windows opening, dogs barking, children crying, and the bathers themselves laughing and swimming far beyond the lagoon, as though pursuing the cloud in an excess of youthful, comic spirits.

Mrs Barnfield got up, dusted her bloomers, and decided she would do no more work that day. She gathered her equipment together and started her journey home, but before she had reached her cottage she wondered if the strange appearance of the cloud, its odd passage through the cones of the volcano, might not have a meaning, some message for herself alone – a message concerned with the fulfilment of her quest. It was then she realized that the cloud had paused and opened above the concealed plateau where the festival had been held – this hidden place unknown to foreigners and forbidden to the Islanders themselves except on those sacred occasions when they gathered together to perform their rituals there.

The idea might be fanciful, as so many of her ideas proved to be; the incident might have no meaning at all – and yet it might be most indicative, most revealing. At any rate, she determined to explore both the cave and the plateau with its little grove, and as she went there next morning, as soon as her household tasks were completed, she kept nodding her head and saying vigorously to herself, 'We'll see! ... We'll wait and see!'

For the next month she thoroughly explored the possibilities of the place. She found only a few broken tablets, which she regarded contemptuously now, having seen so many of them; but she gathered them together and returned them to the volcano. She had almost abandoned her search of that locality as worthless, when one morning, against one of the small hills, her pick broke through so unexpectedly that she staggered forward and fell to her knees. It was the narrow entrance to a small, cool cave, and when she had cleared away the debris and entered, there before her eyes was her major find – the find which, somehow, she had always known she sought; and at once she put down her pick and wept with nervous excitement.

When she recovered she catalogued her discoveries in her mind: there were dozens of scrolls which must, at one time, have been finely-worked skin, but which had solidified now into black, conical masses as hard as stone, there were many clay tablets in perfect condition, their writing still plainly visible; there were a dozen slabs of what seemed to be alabaster, with delicate, minute writing incised on their surfaces. They rested alone, apart from the other things, in a carved stone box, and while she did not know their significance she knew they had, at one time, been of overwhelming importance to others.

Then, as she examined her finds in silence, her mind went back to the book Mr Hansen had lent her – to the story she had read there of the attack on the Island that had destroyed its civilization. Perhaps on that terrible, remote day, some High Priest had hidden these sacred things in this place that he alone knew. Perhaps he had died in the general slaughter, without revealing the place of concealment, and thus the treasures of Shurabast had lain concealed all these centuries, awaiting her discovering hand.

In addition to those objects containing writing, the one which had attracted her attention first, there were two others which did not seem to belong in a library at all: they were a cup and spoon, and they were made of some transparent and polished stone; perhaps rock crystal.

For a long time she examined the objects she had found, impressing the identity of each on her mind; but in the days that followed she carried those that contained writing to the volcano and returned them to Rahabaat, just as she had done with her lesser discoveries.

The cup and spoon, since they seemed entirely harmless, were, she decided, too useful to be destroyed: the practical side of her nature prevented so petulant an act, for she felt that, divorced of their heathen associations, and washed well with soap and hot water, she could easily put them to some Christian, everyday use of her own choosing.

With this, her major find, she felt that her accounts were closed, her mission fulfilled. She put her implements away in the storehouse, took off her uniforms, and turned again to the management of her house and the care of her husband, as though awakening vigorously from a most rewarding dream.

All this happened in the early summer of the eighth year of her residence on October Island, and looking back, Mrs Barnfield was surprised that time had passed so quickly: already she was fifty-one years old, and a middle-aged woman! Her husband had long since passed his sixty-sixth birthday. He was an old man by any standard, she felt.

Chapter Twelve

NOT long afterwards, the natives of October Island, to the astonishment of the Reverend Barnfield and his wife Irma, and no doubt to the equal astonishment of themselves, were won for the Gospel Prophets in a mass conversion which was regarded later by the Board of Ordained Bishops as a true miracle – as perhaps it was. The thing came about most unexpectedly, and although Mrs Barnfield later understood some of the factors involved, her husband never did, which, she felt, was quite satisfactory from both her viewpoint and the viewpoint of the converts.

It happened one afternoon just prior to the summer arrival of the *Mattie B. Powell*. The father of the Radja's eldest wife had come down with a most peculiar sickness. He wouldn't move off his mats and he would take no food except a little coconut milk at night and morning. 'I do wish there was something we could do for him,' said Mrs Barnfield. 'That coconut milk isn't at all nourishing. He's going to get himself into a serious state, if he goes on this way.'

She went into her kitchen, wondering how best to aid the old man. Then, all at once, she had an idea of a sort, and she came back into the living-room and said, 'There are several cans of condensed milk left over from the last trip of the *Mattie B* ... Now, condensed milk is very nourishing, with all that sugar and everything in it. It must be greatly more sustaining than coconut milk.'

Sam nodded, and she went on to say that condensed milk was easy to administer; and it couldn't possibly do the old man any harm, even if it failed to help him very much. Sam agreed that this was true enough, and Mrs Barnfield went into her kitchen and opened one of the remaining cans.

But she did not want to serve the milk out of the tin itself, as that method, while adequate for the informal meals of herself and Mr Barnfield, would hardly be courteous where a guest was concerned; so she emptied the can into the ceremonial cup she had found in the cave, put in the spoon that accompanied the cup, and went back to her husband to show him what she had done.

Together they went to the sick man, and Sam knelt beside him, and speaking in a soothing voice he said they had come to aid him in his sickness. Then he lifted the man's indifferent head and Irma put a spoonful of the milk between his lips. He took it willingly enough, but when he caught sight of the cup that held it, and the spoon that offered it, he sprang up from his mats, his strength remarkably restored to him, and ran outside shouting in a hysterical voice: '*Rubo-aam! Rubo-aam! Manoa pono el Ok-tur-baat, rubo-aam!*'

For a time there was complete silence, and then the cry was taken up from Islander to Islander, from house to house, from village to village, from hilltop to hilltop. It was the only sound heard on the Island, but it was heard everywhere; and then suddenly it stopped as oddly as it had begun.

The sick man's family had come out at once, and when they heard his story and saw the cup in Mrs Barnfield's hands, they fell to their knees and touched their foreheads to the dust. Mrs Barnfield stood in puzzlement, not quite knowing what was expected of her; but she gave each a taste of the milk, and when the cup was exhausted Sam opened the remaining cans and brought them to her. She refilled her cup as long as there was milk to offer, and when there was none, she offered the spoon symbolically. It was at this point that the Reverend Barnfield realized that a miracle had occurred before his eyes, and raising his arm towards the skies, he preached to the people.

A great congregation gathered to hear him, and this time nobody ran away. Afterwards, at his instruction, the people made a confession of faith, as he instructed them to, and he received them all into the ranks of the Gospel Prophets. That night he began his famous report of the conversion of October Island. He worked on it each night thereafter for a week, and when the *Mattie B. Powell* arrived it was ready for mailing in Honolulu.

Afterwards, both the Reverend Barnfield and his wife Irma were content, feeling that their individual missions had been accomplished. It was at this time that they began thinking of leaving the Island, of returning home again. Mrs Barnfield would sometimes speak of the friends she had once known, wondering which of them were now living, and which were dead, and as she moved about her house, or sat rocking on her veranda, she

130

sometimes visualized her return, which she always saw as a pleasant visit only – an interlude in her residence on October Island, to which she must inevitably return when the visit was ended – and she smiled gently, seeing a great gathering of her loved ones, all those she had cherished and once held dear, there at the station to greet her.

Her husband's desire for his homeland was more focused in its aim, more intense in its origin; and sometimes at night, when he knelt to say his prayers he would find his lips saying instead, 'Dear Lord, if I could only be cold once more! If I could only hear sleighbells again, or see snow.' Then, to his astonishment, he would find himself weeping, his face pressed flat against the mattress of his bed. It was almost as if he were passing through some delayed and inappropriate change of life, and that the object of his fading desires was not the conventional, warm-bodied young girl, but the granite contours, the cold, spinsterish charm of his native Vermont.

They were closer together during these weeks than they had ever been, and in the evenings, as Mrs Barnfield sewed or played her melodeon, he talked of his past to her, sometimes following her from room to room. During this period he went earnestly about his tasks, rising at daybreak so that he would miss none of the day's precious hours, preaching, instruction his converts in creed and ritual, and baptizing them, when he felt they were ready for baptism, in the pool behind the Radja's kampong; and then, as though the rigours of conversion had exhausted the last of his strength, he collapsed while delivering one of his sermons, and his followers brought him home and put him to bed.

In the long illness that followed, Mrs Barnfield took his place as best she could: preaching – although ineptly, she thought – placating, instructing, cooperating, and making herself useful to her beloved friends, who, in turn, loved her so dearly. She was greatly worried about her husband, seeing him lying so white and weak in the house, unable even to raise his hand: she thought he would surely die this time, but he did not, and in the early autumn he was able to sit on the veranda, and later to rest again on the terrace in his old place: to receive his converts there, to give them his blessing, and to receive in return their avowals of devotion and faith.

When he was a little stronger, when it appeared he would survive this illness, too, Mrs Barnfield discussed with him, as tactfully as she could manage it, their departure from the Island, not in fantasy, as they had done before, but in reality. He would not hear of it. He closed his eyes; he shook his head stubbornly; he pointed out that he was a soldier in the service of the Lord, and that soldiers remained at their posts until they perished, or were recalled. If it were God's will that he die in this remote place of heat, smell, and opulent colour, then he must accept that, as he had accepted all other hazards when he had entered the ministry.

Mrs Barnfield tried arguing with him, pointing out that the Governing Board could hardly recall him unless they knew that he wanted to be recalled, particularly now that he had written such a remarkable page in their religious history. They probably thought him content to remain on October Island – and why shouldn't they think so with no information to the contrary? . . . She sat beside him and turned his head so that he was forced to look directly into her eyes. 'Did you even mention your illness in your report to the Governing Board?' she asked. 'Have you at any time reported how ill you've been recently?'

'No, I have not,' he said. 'The Governing Board has more important matters to consider than the state of my health. Now, will you please leave me alone?'

'No, Mr Barnfield, I will not leave you alone. It's most necessary for us to discuss these matters. I know how badly you want to go home again, and there's no reason why you shouldn't, with your work completed here.' Then, irritated a little at his unreasonable nature, she stamped her foot in exasperation, and said, 'And please don't pretend that you're the victim and I'm the persecutor, for it's simply not true. As far as I'm concerned I'm content to remain on October Island for ever. It's your well-being I'm thinking of. I have a duty to perform that I'm quite conscious of: my duty is to look after you and see that you come to no harm through your own obstinacy. I mean to perform that duty to the best of my ability.'

He sighed and said, 'I've never questioned your fidelity, Mrs Barnfield. But your nature is one thing and mine is another. I must abide by my nature and not yours. I hope that closes the conversation.'

132

She said, 'Very well, Mr Barnfield!' got up, and went into her house; but the issue was by no means closed in her mind, and as she stood there in her kitchen, preparing the broth for her husband's luncheon, she planned her next moves: she would write a letter to the Governing Board telling them of Mr Barnfield's desperate condition and of his determination not to quit the Island until he was ordered to do so. She would ask that they keep her letter confidential as her husband was a proud, severe man; but if they saw fit to make the recall, she requested that they give some reason other than his health for doing so. She shaped the letter in her mind, adding, eliminating, clarifying, and polishing; and when the *Mattie B. Powell* came on her December trip, it was addressed and ready in its envelope.

She hurried with it to the harbour and arrived there as the schooner was being moored. There was a surprise awaiting her, one which she had not anticipated, for Mr Hansen was back on the *Mattie B.*, not as mate this time, but as her captain. He saw her approaching and he ran down the beach to meet her, his hands extended in welcome. He explained that he had tired at last of wandering and that he had returned to Honolulu, that being the city he liked best of all those he had seen. He'd been back in Hawaii for several months now, working around the docks; then, as it happened, the old master of the schooner had been transferred to a better command and the owners had offered him the captaincy of the *Mattie B.* since he knew both the ship and her trade so well.

She held his hand warmly as he talked, and looking intently into his face she thought how greatly he had changed in the years since she had last seen him. Already his hair was turning; he would be grey early she thought. There were lines in his dark-skinned, pensive face which had not been there before. Even his manner had changed, for now he regarded people warily, his grey eyes narrowed and on guard.

He asked her to come on deck and sit with him, as before, while he supervised discharge of the cargo, and she did so; then, remembering her letter, she gave it to him, explaining its contents and the circumstances that had made it necessary. They talked for a time of trivial things, but all the while Captain Hansen wanted to ask the question that was first in his mind – the question concerning the conversion of the October Islanders, for already, even in the short time of its accomplishment, it had become famous in the neighbouring islands.

He had heard of it first in an establishment in Honolulu, for there a plump, sedate young woman had entertained her patrons with a song which she called 'Condensed Milk Salvation'. The girl had sung softly, to the swishing accompaniment of the two small, sand-filled gourds she held in her hands; and when she had finished her audience made kissing sounds with their lips, laughed gently, and leaned back against their mats.

Captain Hansen, recalling the scene, wanted now to determine the facts, to discover, if he could, which of the song's allegations were fanciful and which true; then, as though the matter had just come to mind, he asked the question casually. Mrs Barnfield looked at him steadily, and then glancing down at the deck she plucked nervously at her skirt. She raised her eyes after a moment, and feeling that she could trust him not to reveal her secret, she said, 'There's a certain matter I've wanted to tell somebody for a long time, and I feel that you're the one person in the world to hear my confession. I wanted to speak of it to you before, but I didn't have the courage, I suppose.'

She began at the beginning. She told of the discovery of the first of the prayer stones, and how, persevering in her efforts, she had made her final, overwhelming find. She told how she had destroyed the other things but had saved the cup and spoon. She described the chalice in circumstantial detail, while Captain Hansen made an odd sound with his lips, laughed, or shook his head in disbelief. She related the illness of the Radja's father-in-law and how she and her husband had offered the old man condensed milk out of the cup.

At this point Captain Hansen bent forward excitedly and said, 'Will you tell me what happened next?'

She did so, and Captain Hansen raised his hands helplessly in the air, laughed, and said, 'Do you know who the people thought you were?'

'Why, of *course* I know!' said Mrs Barnfield indignantly. 'I read that book you lent me about the legends of October Island, so I was prepared, in a way. In fact, I'd known for a long time that the people regarded me as some sort of supernatural being, which was all right with me, as it most certainly didn't hurt anybody for them to think so. In fact, I must confess that I encouraged them a little ... But when they acted in such a peculiar manner about the cup, I came to the conclusion that they mistook me for that virgin priestess who was to lead them to another age of peace and glory. Well, I let them think so. It may have been wrong of me, but personally, I can't see what difference it makes.'

'Do you know what the cup was?' asked Captain Hansen. 'Do you know what it represented?'

'Well, not at first; and I'm not too sure even now. But by putting two and two together, by listening to the prayers of the High Priest and asking that nice-looking young Brenan-Oan some discreet questions, I realize it's somehow connected with the youth of Rahabaat.'

Captain Hansen said that the cup she had found was the cup that Rahabaat had fashioned with his own hands from the skull of his divine, cannibal mother. It was from this cup that Rahabaat, and through him, Shurabast, had drawn its power. The cup had been lost for thousands of years, but its memory had persisted, and its restoration to the people was, in their mind, the most important thing that could possibly have happened to them.

She nodded gravely, and said that while she understood these things her husband did not. 'In fact,' she said, 'Mr Barnfield doesn't realize to this day the circumstances of the sudden conversion. He only knows that God somehow placed a great instrument for good in our hands, and he feels, as I do, that we should make the most of it.'

'Well, that seems sensible,' said Captain Hansen after a moment.

Mrs Barnfield said, 'In so far as I'm concerned personally, I don't see how it makes the slightest difference one way or another so long as the October Islanders were converted to God. The main thing was to induce them to abandon their heathen ways, and that we have done. Anyway, even if there was some slight deception in their conversion, everybody is now content with the way things turned out – the Islanders, Mr Barnfield, and myself.'

The new mate came up for a moment to discuss a point which had arisen with reference to the water casks. When it was settled, Captain Hansen turned again to his guest and asked her to continue her story. She said, 'There isn't much that you don't already know. But I must admit that giving the milk became a bit of a nuisance later on. You see, I'd made a bargain: I'd consented to administer the milk from the cup if the High Priest would instruct the natives to be baptized by Mr Barnfield, and naturally I had to keep my end of the agreement; but there were so many ceremonials they expected me to participate in, some of them quite strange, I assure you. For instance, the milk must be given at sunset, and then only in that grove of trees at the base of Min-Rahabaat. Of course, they always sent a chair for me, so it wasn't too inconvenient; but I must stand in just such a way during the rites, and I must hold the cup and spoon in the correct hands, at the right distance from the altar, and, of course, say the traditional words. Luckily I was never one to bother too much about religious precedent, so I agreed to all the reasonable demands the congregation made on me.'

'How about the Reverend Barnfield? Did he make objections or did he agree to these things too?'

'Frankly, Captain Hansen, he didn't know too much about it.' Mrs Barnfield laughed, looked down apologetically, and added, 'Mr Barnfield has been sick a great deal, as I told you ... But even when he's well, he doesn't know what's going on half the time. I'm not criticizing him, Captain Hansen, but you know that as well as I do.'

Captain Hansen nodded gravely, and Mrs Barnfield, brought back to the purpose of her visit, reminded him once more of the letter she had written, asking him again to mail it personally, on the first fast steamer from Honolulu. 'He's a very sick and a very stubborn man, and it's almost impossible to do anything with him. But I mean to take him back to Vermont and bury him where he wants to be buried. I only hope he manages to survive until the *Mattie B.* comes back on her next trip.'

When she had gone, Captain Hansen went to his stateroom to think over the things he had just heard. He kicked off his shoes and stretched himself out on his bunk, his arms folded beneath his head. The words the sick man had used when he ran out of his hut were in the fifth, or sacred, language of the Island. Translated, they were: 'She is here! She is here! The Great Breast Mother of the World is here!'

He turned on his belly and laughed for the first time in weeks. He laughed hysterically, his mouth pressed flat against his pillow, for he wondered at that moment if the missionaries had actually converted the people of October Island as they imagined, or if they, themselves, had not unwittingly embraced Shurabast. Later, when he was calm once more, he washed his face and hands and went back on deck, in time to see his guest reach the small peninsular of palms, hesitate there, look back, and then pass beyond the range of his vision.

She walked slowly, sorting the mail as she went along. There was a Christmas present for Sam that trip. Later she gave him the package, excitedly telling him all the while that Mr Hansen was on the *Mattie B. Powell* again. He turned the package over and over in his fumbling, uncertain hands, as though undecided what to do with it. The present was from his sister. He had not heard from her in years, and, really, he had no reason to hear from her now, since their lives had long since drifted apart; but when they were children they had been close in spirit. She had long since married, and he knew that she had had a large family. Perhaps her children were all married too; perhaps she was as lonely as he was; perhaps her thoughts now turned to him for comfort, at the twilight of her life ...

'Mr Barnfield! Mr Barnfield!' said Irma. She laughed a little and added, 'Why don't you open your present and see what it is?'

It was three bars of pink, scented soap called 'Rose Blush'. The bars rested in a nest of fragrant, paper lace. Each bar had its individual, silver wrapper, with a pink but badly printed, rose, as though someone had jogged the printer's elbow at the instant the die came down.

A letter accompanied the gift, and in it his sister recalled a conversation they had had as children, a conversation which he, by closing his eyes and concentrating with all his might, dimly remembered too: it seemed they had been together in the village a few days before Christmas, and while waiting inside the general store for their father to make his purchases for the farm, they had examined the gifts that others, although not themselves, would receive. On the counter were gift-boxes of this same soap, a soap which Sam had not remembered seeing since that distant day. Behind the gift-boxes a big cardboard rose bush lifted high above the counter, and bore not roses on its branches but cakes of soap marked Rose Blush, while beneath the bush were those bars which, having attained a maximum ripeness, had presumably detached themselves from the parent stem and now awaited gathering by the benign firm of Weatherford & Petrie, whose advertised goal was to bring the luxuries of dukes and duchesses to those of moderate circumstances – to serve and scent mankind rather than to make a profit from his cleanliness.

Part of these things were stated in his sister's letter, part he remembered himself. But he had forgotten, and still could not recall, the remark his sister attributed to him on that day so long ago: it seemed that both had been admiring the soap and wishing they could have a cake of it for their own, when Sam said earnestly, 'When you're rich, Mabel, give me a bar, and I'll think of you each week when I use it ...'

The gift and the letter brought back to him all the sadness of his youth, all the desperation of the poverty he had known. Tears came to his eyes, for he was sentimental these days and easily moved. He approached his wife where she sat in the summerhouse and read the letter to her. He said, 'I remember that Christmas very well, now that Mabel has reminded me of it. I got a new pair of stockings that year. That was all. My father had my shoes soled too, but I never counted that as a Christmas present.'

'You mean not even an apple and orange? Not even candy, or dates? That was a slim Christmas for a child, I must say.'

'We were very poor,' said Sam. 'When I look back, I don't see how we managed to get along. But we did, somehow.'

'We were in moderate circumstances, I suppose,' said Irma thoughtfully. 'Anyway, we certainly had enough of everything all the time. But of course Papa was disagreeable.'

Sam said, 'It was very cold that Christmas. It must have been below zero that day when Mabel and I looked at the soap. I remember the cold best of all. The mud in the road would freeze until it was like iron. Then later it would snow, and the snow would stay all winter, sometimes. I can see people passing the store window with steam coming out of their mouths and noses, hugging themselves and hurrying as much as they could.'

'I prefer a warmer climate, personally,' said Mrs Barnfield.

'We had only this one iron stove in the house,' said Sam. 'It didn't warm us too much, but we'd all huddle around it when we weren't in the kitchen. When we got up in the morning – I slept in the attic with my three elder brothers – it was so cold that you could almost take the cold in your two hands and break

138

it. Water froze in the pitcher, and once the pitcher cracked. After that, we had to empty the pitcher at night.'

'It sounds very disagreeable, Mr Barnfield.'

'The wind would cut through you like a knife,' said Sam. 'If you got off the path, likely as not you'd sink in a snowdrift up to your waist. People passing down the road on their way to the village bent almost double against the wind, it was so cold and bitter. Their faces were red and rough, but they were so wrapped up against the cold you could only see their eyes, and a little piece of their foreheads.'

'It doesn't sound at all attractive to me, Mr Barnfield.'

'I can remember my father coming home with ice clinging to his beard and eyebrows. You have no idea how cold it could be in those days.'

'I know what cold weather is like. I know well indeed. But personally I prefer a milder climate, the climate here on October Island, for instance.'

The Reverend Barnfield said, 'When my brothers and I went to the barn to take care of the livestock, the cold was sometimes so bitter that it was like a hand snatching your breath away. You had to be careful, or your ears, or even your hands and feet, would freeze.'

'Don't forget that I was reared in northern Pennsylvania, and, that isn't exactly in the tropics, Mr Barnfield. When the winter breezes blew off Lake Erie – well, it was most disagreeable I assure you.'

'I remember a man who got lost and froze to death. I used to know his name but I've forgotten it long ago. He was related to the Calvert family. He was a young, handsome man. He was anxious to get home, as his bride was afraid to stay alone at night, so he turned off the road, and took a short cut, but those who loved him never saw him alive again. Next day, I saw him lying dead in McDaniel's field. You'd think his legs would be drawn up, or his face twisted, but they weren't. He was stretched out serenely at full length. He looked so contented there, with his hands crossed on his breast, and his eyes open and looking up at the sky, the way they had frozen. His face was white and pure, like something carved out of the finest marble. There was a little smile at the corners of his mouth ... Oh, but he must have been very cold, indeed!'

He talked on and on, and Irma, knowing how sick at heart he was, how greatly he despised this hot place where it seemed he must die and be buried, humoured him as best as she could. But she had other duties too, for as the weeks passed, and she grew more and more confident that the letter of recall would arrive on the next voyage of the *Mattie B.*, she began to make her plans for an immediate departure. She made a bonfire on the beach and burned all those useless possessions which accumulate everywhere, and when the blaze was going well, she threw on it the tracts and pamphlets which they had brought with them for the instruction of the natives, but which they had never used. She destroyed old clothing which neither she nor her husband would ever wear again. She scoured her store room, and put it in order. She made a list of the things she would take with her, and the things she would leave behind: she would take with her as little as possible, she would leave behind as much as she could, including all the furniture, in the event she should be able to return.

Then, shortly before the schooner was due again, she called the Radja, the High Priest, and Brenan-Oan, into conference, and told them her plans. Her husband was dying, she said, and she must take him back to his native land. Parting with her friends would be a terrible blow, even for a short time, but it seemed inevitable.

'You will return to us?' said the High Priest in alarm. 'You will surely come to us again?'

'I will return unless the difficulties are insurmountable. It will be hard to arrange, I know, but I'll manage it somehow. I'm not a woman who's easily thwarted.'

'How long will you be away from us?' asked the Radja.

'I'll return as soon as my duty is done,' said Mrs Barnfield. 'I will not remain away from you one hour longer than is necessary.'

'You will return to us alone?' asked Brenan-Oan.

Mrs Barnfield thought a moment, and then said, 'Yes. If I return at all, I will return alone.'

Her friends seemed so depressed, so downcast at her departure, that she added: 'There's one thing you can do to speed my return, and that is to *pray* for it! I'm a firm believer in the power of prayer, and of course I'll be praying constantly, too, that I be

140

returned to you. But remember, you must do your part as well. When I have gone, you must instruct all my loved ones here on October Island to pray for me. If they pray with devotion and earnestness of purpose, our joint prayers will surely be granted.'

Chapter Thirteen

THE letter Mrs Barnfield waited for was aboard the schooner when she arrived at October Island in the summer of 1903. It stated that inasmuch as the Barnfields had laboured so long and earnestly in the foreign field, it had been decided to recall them for conference, and, perhaps, reassignment elsewhere. This could be determined later, but first, it was desired that they enjoy a vacation in their native land, renewing those old ties which, of necessity, had lapsed with the years.

It was requested that they sail immediately for home, preferably on the ship that brought this letter, since plans for their reception were already being made in San Francisco.

Mrs Barnfield listened to the letter, and said, 'Captain Hansen has another port to make before returning to Hawaii. I'll ask him to stop here again, on his way back, and pick us up. We'll be ready then.'

'We must follow instructions,' said Sam. 'We must leave at once, I suppose.'

'Yes,' said Irma. 'I suppose we must.'

The words became a sort of refrain for her during the days that followed, and she moved about in a world of operatic unreality, surrounded by the friends she must leave behind. She smiled encouragingly to all those who came for her final blessing, and said, 'I'll be back. I'll manage it some way. You'll see ... But pray for me! Pray for my return earnestly! Pray constantly!'

She was a little depressed during those final, trying days, but once aboard the schooner, she was her old self again. She had determined, at least during the initial part of her journey home, to relax and enjoy a holiday at sea, but she was unhappy in her idleness, and third day out, she asked Captain Hansen to bring her his clothes, and the clothes of the members of his crew, that needed repairing; and seated placidly on deck, in the place she had selected as the most comfortable for her needs, she worked methodically.

It was a dull day, with rain threatening, and perhaps a squall later on. The sea and the heavens were the same dull grey; and

142

with low clouds scurrying above, in the sky, and waves lifting and running beneath, in the sea, the horizon had disappeared, and the schooner seemed caught in a vast globe of watery light from which it could never escape.

Presently Captain Hansen approached. He had a piece of soft pine in his hand, and, as though to mask his intentions, he opened his knife, and whittled absently. He leaned for a moment against the rail of the schooner, watching the grey, running water; then Mrs Barnfield bit off a thread, looked up from her task, and said, 'There are several things I want to ask you, but this is the first chance I've had, as I didn't like to discuss the matters I have in mind in Mr Barnfield's presence.'

She hesitated, feeling that her questions called for both tact and proper timing, and then said, 'In the letter you wrote me from Chicago, you mentioned a young lady of exceptional personal charm: Miss Dilustro, your dancing partner, to be precise. Now, Captain Hansen, I got the impression you were in love with this girl, and that she was in love with you, although you didn't say so in so many words.'

'You got the right impression,' said Captain Hansen. 'It was true enough.'

'The peculiar thing is,' said Irma, 'that you didn't once mention her name when I saw you on your first return trip to the Island. It occurred to me when I reached home, but I said to myself that I'd talked so much about my letter, and Mr Barnfield's illness, that I hadn't given you a chance to discuss your own affairs. Your silence was explainable on that occasion, but this time we've been together three full days, and you still haven't referred to her.' Then, seeing he was about to interrupt, she added quickly, 'Tell me one thing! – Are you married, or not?'

'No,' he said. 'I'm not married.'

'I see,' said Mrs Barnfield. She worked thoughtfully on an enlarged buttonhole, and then added sternly, 'Did you offer Miss Dilustro marriage?'

'Yes, a number of times.'

'And she *refused* you?' said Mrs Barnfield in surprise. She laughed bleakly, and continued, 'Miss Dilustro is a most peculiar girl, is all I can say.'

He continued his whittling in silence, and after a moment Mrs

Barnfield went on, 'Tell me, if you don't mind, just what did happen to your romance.'

Nothing at all had happened, he said. He had merely assumed too much, had taken too much for granted. He had fallen in love with Miss Dilustro at once, and she had been in love with him, too. Nobody could ever convince him to the contrary. He had wanted to marry her, but she'd refused him over and over, for reasons of her own. That had created an impossible situation, as Mrs Barnfield could surely see, and he'd come to the conclusion, at length, that there was nothing to do but separate from her. This he had done. He'd simply left her a note, and walked out one night, and that was that. Perhaps he'd acted like a sulking child in the matter, but he'd not even bothered to tell her good-bye. He'd spent the next year in New York, mostly in libraries, filling in some of the gaps in his education.

Mrs Barnfield nodded vigorously and said his conduct seemed entirely logical to her. There was silence for a time, and then both turned their heads at the sound of footsteps. It was only Sam Barnfield coming across the deck, walking cautiously. He looked about him, nodded, and then, going to the rail of the schooner, he stared down at the dark, lifting water. Captain Hansen watched him in pity, wondering what thoughts were in his stricken mind that made his face pucker with despair, his hands tremble against the rail of the ship; then moving away slowly, he came up to Irma Barnfield, and sat in the chair beside her.

'Go on with what you were saying,' said Mrs Barnfield. 'He's so deaf, you almost have to shout to make him hear you these days.'

He sighed and lowered his head, since his was the melancholy of those who are neither one thing nor the other. Once, long ago, he had lived with some assurance; but as the years receded, and the cleavage in his nature became more and more apparent, he saw nothing about him but sadness, as if a deep pathos, for his kind, was the essence of life itself, the background against which we are born, and struggle, and live out our lives to the ends.

Mrs Barnfield said, 'Oh, very well, if you don't want to tell me!' She laughed and turned back to her mending. 'You'll tell me some day, when you're in the right mood. I can wait.'

Captain Hansen went on with his carving, which was taking the form of a shark with widespread, predatory jaws. There was, indeed, a great deal that he had not told Irma Barnfield, and would never tell her, or anybody else. The confessional did not come easy for him ... Carmen was all he had ever wanted in a woman, and for a time he thought happiness was surely his. He was jealous of the other men who admired her, of all those other people who, through the very nature of her profession, must occupy a place in her life, for he had lived with her as her husband almost from the time they had first met. He had wanted her for himself, and for himself alone, and in the first week of their union he had asked her to marry him. She shook her head, smiled seductively, and said, 'Why rush things? We've got plenty of time for that later on.'

'But why shouldn't we get married now? Why put it off? The act is doing all right, and we can afford it. Why wait any longer?'

'Marriage is such a serious matter, Axel. It's something you got to think about a long time. Marriage isn't something you rush into. It's a sacrament. Ask anybody, and they'll tell you the same.'

'But what about the way we're living now? Is that a sacrament, too?'

'Oh, this is something else. This isn't important, like marriage.'

'It seems important to me.'

'Oh, quit being so stubborn and intense. Let's go rehearse that new number. I want to show you the dance steps again. You haven't quite got it down the way it should be.'

He had persisted in his plea that she marry him, and at last he discovered the true reasons of her refusal: her family were old music hall and circus people, and they were straight-laced, she said. They all lived in a small town in Indiana, and she'd live there too, when she retired from the stage ... And what if she married a Hawaiian, and brought him home, and introduced him to her folks? Of course, she didn't have any feelings about these matters, but her mother would never speak to her again! Her sisters, and her friends, would simply pretend that she didn't exist any more! Her father would probably break her neck! Oh, no! Marriage would not work out at all for them! It was better to let things go along the way they were – certainly for the time being.

'I'm not a Hawaiian. I'm an October Islander.'

'It's the same thing. Now, don't try to throw me off the track, Axel. You know what I mean, as well as I do.'

'I don't know what you mean at all; or at least I'm trying *not* to know what you mean.'

'Now, darling, don't sulk and act that way. You know I love you. Don't I do everything I can to make you happy? Do I so much as look at another man? Do I nag you, or spend all your money, the way other women do? All right then! – Isn't that enough? Why do you want to marry me, and ruin my life?'

'How do you expect me to be a man, when you abase me, and deflate my pride so greatly?'

She came to him quickly and threw herself into his arms, kissing him passionately, her body pressed sensuously against his own. 'Don't!' she said. 'Don't confuse me again with those big words you see!' She cried, and pressed her face against his breast. 'You know I love you,' she said. 'It would kill me if anything parted us ... My God, what else do you expect of me?'

He sighed, and left it that way for the time being, making excuses to himself for the insularity of her friends, and for the narrowness of her own mind, hoping that somehow her viewpoint would change, although he knew quite well that it would not. He was conscious that Mrs Barnfield was speaking again, and he looked up from his work and gave her his full attention.

'Mr Barnfield!' she called out. 'Are you all right? Are you warm enough? I think you'd better sit down, before you tire yourself out.'

Sam turned slowly, a vacant expression on his face. He was in pain at that moment, but hearing himself addressed so peremptorily, he summoned all his will-power, and said that he was perfectly comfortable. Then, staring again at the dark, uplifting sea, he said in a weak voice, as though repeating his report to the Governing Board of Ordained Bishops: 'When we first went to October Island, my wife and I knew that many missionaries had been there before us, and that they'd accomplished nothing at all. For many years the natives resisted us, too. Oh, they were courteous and considerate enough. They were kind and gentle and unassuming on all occasions; but when I tried to preach to them, to show them the way to happiness and divine peace, they would laugh, nudge one another, and perhaps ridicule me under their breaths.'

His voice faltered, and he passed his hands roughly across his face, as if to brush something away from him. He had read somewhere that men buried at sea did not sink to the bottom: instead, they found the particular level in the bed of the ocean where the weight of their bodies coincided with some intricate displacement of water, and thus remained suspended there, neither buried nor unburied, for all time. He shuddered.

Mrs Barnfield, lowering her voice a little, as though to exclude her husband from the conversation, went into a minute description of her search for the antiquities of October Island. Captain Hansen, although he nodded gravely, and asked the appropriate question when it was needed, heard little that she said, for his mind was concerned again with his own past, particularly with that final, abrupt episode which had ended his association with Carmen for ever.

In the seventh month of their union, she had confessed in a burst of tears that she was pregnant. He had been quite happy at the turn their love affair had taken, for it seemed to him that marriage was now inevitable, and that the sooner it was arranged, the better it would be for all concerned.

'You're so dull about these things!' she cried out in a desperate voice. 'So lacking in understanding. Or maybe you do understand, but pretend you don't to make me unhappy.'

'What is it I don't understand?'

'We've been through all that, Axel. You know why I can't marry you. I thought that was all settled. We've got to figure out some other way of handling things.'

'I haven't any objections to marrying *you*.'

'But it isn't the same thing. You know that as well as I do. I'm an American. Why should you have any objection to marrying me? You're talking foolishly, darling.'

'You don't love me very much. If you loved me, you'd want to marry me. That's simple.'

She pulled him down to the bed beside her, and wept without restraint. 'Oh, how can you say a cruel thing like that, Axel? – Of course, I love you. If I didn't love you more than anybody in the world, I wouldn't be in the fix I'm in right now. I wouldn't be living with you openly, and taking chances on people finding out about us.' She released him, and lay back against the pillow, her hands pressed over her eyes, her body quivering with grief.

'Don't ever say again that I don't love you,' she said. 'Don't say it even in fun. You know how much I love you.'

'But not enough to marry me.'

She got up and strode dramatically about the room. 'I can't,' she said. 'I can't. You ask too much of me.' Then taking his hand and resting her cheek against it, she said, 'I have so much to put up with as it is, I'd think you'd try to be considerate, and not hurt my feelings at a time like this. But oh, no! You have no consideration at all, Axel. You think of nobody but yourself!'

They had no engagement for the following week, and it was agreed that she go home and talk things over with her mother. He hoped that when she returned, everything would be straightened out; but when she did come back, he learned she had not been home at all, had never really planned to go there: she'd gone instead to an abortionist and when she told him, he thought for a moment that he would kill her. She had wept, she had implored him to see her side of the story, she had clung to him, she had followed him about protesting her undying love; but that night he'd packed his belongings and walked out, without even telling her good-bye . . . Now, looking back, the affair which had once seemed so important to him had fallen into its proper place in the sequences of his life. It did not seem tragic at all now: It seemed sad, unreal, and a little grotesque, instead.

Mrs Barnfield said, 'It's really remarkable how much the people of October Island admired me. They went out of their way to do me honour. Of course, I was flattered, and properly appreciative, and I did what I could to reciprocate the attention shown me, but still it was a most remarkable demonstration of affection and trust.'

She turned to Sam for confirmation, but he only sighed and inclined his head. He raised his face to the sky, and suddenly he knew that death stood there beside him. He trembled at his knowledge, closed his eyes, and spoke soundlessly. 'Dear Lord!' he whispered. 'Do not let me die at sea. Let me be buried among the hills where I was born.' He lowered his head, resting it on the rail of the schooner, between his grey, intense hands, wondering if the faith of Shurabast was as ridiculous as he once had thought it; that if, after all, it were not the first and final belief of all who live. He stared outward at the dark, deceptive sea, and in that interval he experienced a moment of clarity and resignation: it

148

seemed to him, then, that when everything else had gone, hope sometimes remained; but when hope had gone too, then dignity must somehow take its place.

Captain Hansen threw the carving he had worked on over the side of the ship, closed his knife and put it away. It was a strange thing, he thought, a thing he'd never been able to break down into its component emotions, nor to analyse to any conclusion, but many of those who, because of his differences from them, would neither sit at table with him in a restaurant, nor acknowledge him publicly in the presence of others, would, when they were alone with him, and the doors locked, nudge him implacably towards the nearest bed. It was a strange thing, he thought. It was a most peculiar thing . . . In the years since he had left October Island, he had become familiar with every vice, he had participated in every depravity known to man; and he had rejected them all at length, not because he considered them wrong, but because he found them tiresome, so that now, as he approached his middle thirties, he had achieved not corruption, but a kind of impervious and monstrous purity.

The Reverend Barnfield turned from the rail of the schooner, cleared his throat, and said he was not feeling well; that he was going below to lie down. Irma asked if there were anything he needed, anything she could do for him, and when he said there was not, she nodded and said to Captain Hansen, 'I'm coming back to October Island some day. I don't know at the moment how I'll arrange it, but I'll manage. I promised the Islanders I'd manage it, and I will. One should always keep a promise, I feel.'

Lightning stood out against the sky, in a pattern as involved and as perfect as the illuminated nervous system of a man. It disappeared without thunder, and Captain Hansen, looking gravely into Mrs Barnfield's eyes, said he was sure she'd keep her promise. Mrs Barnfield finished her mending, closed her sewing-box, and said, 'I've been thinking a great deal about you lately, Captain Hansen. You've seen all the world that you want to see. No doubt you've had your share of adventures, too; and you've never lacked company, and never will, although yours isn't really an expensive nature, or even a very friendly one. But you are still a young man, with many years ahead of you to be filled in somehow. Now, tell me what plans you've made for the future.'

He said that the one thing he wanted now was to own and

command his schooner. As it happened, the *Mattie B. Powell* could be bought cheaply from her owners, who had never really known the proper trades to put her in. A four-masted schooner of her quality must have cost around seventy-five thousand dollars to build; and she was only ten years old, at that – as sound as the day her keel was laid. Anybody with cash could have her for about fifteen thousand dollars, say eighteen thousand at the outside. He could see her possibilities, the things that could be done by an owner-captain who knew how to cut corners, how to tramp her to the best advantage. He'd turned the possibilities over and over in his mind. He'd love to have her for his own, although he realized there was small chance of his achieving such an ambitious goal without capital, and without influential friends to help him.

She chided him for his lack of faith. She would join her prayers to his own, she promised, and perhaps God would see fit to grant their plea in time – particularly if they could somehow convince Him that the schooner, if given, would be used in a furtherance of His Power and Glory.

He said, 'Perhaps so. Perhaps so.'

Mrs Barnfield got up from her seat, saying she'd better go below and see if her husband needed anything; but she hesitated, and turning to him again, she said, 'You'd better give me your business address in Honolulu, where you can be reached at once, if I should want to communicate with you.'

He wrote out the address for her, and she read it, folded it, and tucked it away in her sewing-box for safe keeping.

Chapter Fourteen

THE Barnfields sat together on deck discussing plans for their future. After a moment, Irma shifted her chair, shielded her eyes from the glare, and surveyed the monotonously moving sea, on which the sun's rays shimmered and lifted in a dance of golden, refracted light. She had finished her mending for that morning, and as it was now close to lunch time, she folded the garments she had worked on, piled them on the deck beside her, and patted them possessively with her palm. The gesture made her think of the October Islanders, and the difficulties she had once met with in clothing them; and now, looking back, she wondered at her tourist earnestness of those remote days, her concern with such trivial matters.

She said, 'I keep thinking about the Islanders, and how greatly they esteem me. They're quite sweet and gentle, despite some obvious faults.'

Her husband did not answer, and she went on, 'We've been gone a week, at most, but already I miss them, and keep wondering if they miss me, too.' She closed her eyes and abandoned herself to the somnolent rolling and dipping of the ship; then she got up from her chair, smoothed down her dress, and added indignantly, as though Sam had challenged her words, 'Of course they miss me, too! They miss me dreadfully, after all the things I did for them!'

She was right in her surmise, for the people of October Island missed her a great deal indeed, and at the very moment she was speaking, they were taking the most practical means at their command to bring her back again. They had missed her even on that first day when the grey, dirty schooner receded slowly into the immensity of the Pacific Ocean, and they had stood in desolation among the palm trees, wondering when she would return to them. Time, in the eyes of gods, meant little: to Rahabaat, as they well knew, a thousand years was only the lifting of an eyelid, or the turning of a bored wrist; but they were not gods, they were poor mortals, and they wanted the prophesy fulfilled in their own space of years, not generations later, when they were dead.

And so they stood lonely and abandoned, that first day, beside the lagoon, unwilling, in this first impact of grief, to return to their homes, or to take up the routine of their lives; and one by one they dropped to their knees, to repeat the prayers the Reverend Barnfield had assured them were instruments for the fulfilment of the deepest wish. Then, to the obbligato of the prayers, others sang hymns. They sang them over and over, until only the tips of the ship's masts were visible in the fading light; but the schooner did not miraculously turn in her course, and speed back to them, as they so confidently expected: instead, she moved on into distance, a toy that disturbed for a time the loneliness of the great ocean.

When there was no sight of the schooner against the horizon, the people went back to their villages, but not without hope. The miracle had not taken place because they lacked that divine faith of which the Reverend Barnfield had spoken so ardently. They would pray harder, they would sing more fervently, they would deny themselves those pleasures of nature about which he had warned them. Afterwards, their days were spent in ruses to outwit Jehovah, in marshalling arguments to convince Him of their devotion and rectitude, or, alternatively, in staging pageants of abasement, to impress on Him their unworthiness of the gift which they prayed he would, nevertheless, grant them.

But at the end of the fifth month, when their throats were hoarse from prayer, when they were weak from fasting, and nervous from the repudiation of those everyday desires of the flesh, they came to the conclusion that no matter how remarkable this magic was in the hands of missionaries, they themselves lacked the skill to make it work.

Not long afterwards, the *Mattie B. Powell* returned to port, and the Radja called to gather what information he could concerning Mrs Barnfield. Captain Hansen told him all he knew: the Reverend Barnfield was weak, but had survived the trip; Mrs Barnfield was in excellent health, as usual, and her spirits were decidedly optimistic. She looked forward to her return to October Island, and often spoke of it. He had been with them during their stay in Honolulu, and had seen them aboard the steamer that took them to San Francisco.

Ordinarily, he would have lost touch with them at shipside, but, as it happened, the Barnfields had become celebrities of a sort, and for a time he, along with the American reading public, had been able to follow not only their landing in San Francisco, but their triumphal flight across the continent, too. It had all happened in this manner: a reporter for one of the Honolulu papers had called for the routine interview, but after Irma Barnfield, who had never been one to underestimate publicity, had whispered the purpose of the trip, he had known at once that it was really the Race Against Death story, a theme tailored to the measurements of the American heart. His feature had been picked up by the California papers, and when the steamer docked, she was met by a vast crowd of people who prayed publicly on the wharves that the Reverend Barnfield survive until he saw his old home again.

The president of a railway placed his private carriage at the disposal of the missionaries, and the long journey across the United States began. Pastors preached sermons in every pulpit; newspaper men wrote editorials; special prayers were heard in the homes of the nation; and the president's carriage stopped everywhere, in order that the admirers of the old couple should have a chance to go aboard, meet them, and speed them on their way. For a time, prayers were compulsory in the schools, with thousands of children asking daily that the journey of the Barnfields be successfully ended.

The Honolulu papers had recorded the progress of the party in detail, and he'd had no trouble in knowing where they were from day to day; then all at once, the Press abandoned them, for another story, on the same theme, came up and pushed the Barnfields out of the newspapers: the story of a little boy for whom a town was arranging Christmas in August, since it seemed doubtful that he would live to celebrate Christmas at its regular time. The last he had heard of the Barnfields, they were in a railway siding near Buffalo, still rushing onward to their destination. He was confident, however, they had arrived at last, and no doubt they were now safely in Vermont.

The Radja sighed, nodded, and took his leave. He had not understood all the implications of Captain Hansen's report, but he had understood enough; and when he was in his village again, he discussed the situation with his advisers. It was now plain to all why their prayers for Mrs Barnfield's return had failed.

'But how could we pray her back *here*?' asked Brenan-Oan

153

crossly. 'How could we, when the preachers, and those other important people, were praying her on *home*!'

The Radja nodded in agreement, and the High Priest wandered away from the others, and sat alone on a palm stump to consider this new turn of circumstance. It wasn't the preachers, or the railway president, or the newspaper editors, that bothered him: It was those thousands of school children praying in concert. It was disheartening, really, for he, more versed than the others in matters of faith, well knew that in a marathon of piety, in a praying tug-of-war of this nature, the plea of innocent children was sure to be given preference; but he was not nearly so pessimistic as the others, and he pointed out that no matter how unskilled their hands were in the new faith they had embraced as an auxiliary faith to Shurabast, they still had Rahabaat to rely upon, to aid them in resolving their calamity; and that afternoon he called a meeting to discuss their future actions.

Now Rahabaat, as everybody knew, was fond of the flesh of plump, young children. If such a child were delivered to him at sunrise each morning, he would in time, when his social debt became too embarrassing to be ignored further, stir himself from his perpetual lethargy for a while, and see that the accompanying prayers of his donors were granted. But the people did not want to sacrifice their greatly loved children if an alternate solution could be found.

They discussed this problem with sighs and shakes of their heads. To give up their children would be a dreadful thing indeed, but, after all, children were easily replaceable, and Mrs Barnfield was not. The loss of a few children, no matter how dearly they were cherished, could hardly be compared with the thousand years of glory that such a sacrifice guaranteed; it was a difficult problem indeed – one which should not be rushed into without thought.

Then Brenan-Oan pointed out most sensibly that since Rahabaat was so old, the chances were he could no longer distinguish between the flesh of a plump child, and the flesh of any other plump, young animal: a nice little pig, for example.

At once the Islanders discussed this way out of their dilemma.

'Brenan-Oan's contention has merit in it,' said the High Priest. 'But first, let us examine the facts, to see if such a plan is possible. Let us examine impartially the similarities that exist between our dear children, and young pigs. When we have done so, and have reached a conclusion, we can then debate the differences that exist between the two. In this way we can have some idea of what Rahabaat, who hasn't our keenness of perception, will think – whether or not he will be taken in by our cleverness.'

'Pigs and children are identical in their disregard of all habits of ordinary daintiness,' said the Radja solemnly. 'Both are born with a hatred of water, and a love of dirt. A pig will wallow in a mudhole all day long, and a child will do the same if its mother turns her head to speak to a neighbour, or to look at the pot boiling on her stove.'

'That is true,' said the others softly. 'That is all too true. Neither a pig nor a child has any regard for cleanliness. It's an established fact. known to all.'

'Both pigs and children are stubborn and unreasonable,' said the chief of the *brunga-brungas*. 'When it comes to my profession, I'd rather treat a pig than a child any day, for if things get too bad, and the pig knocks the medicine out of your hand for the fourth time running, you can always clout it over the nose without having its mother come at you with a washing-stick, screaming, and making a scene from one end of the Island to the other.'

'That is true,' said the others. 'We've all seen such occurrences.'

The High Priest said, 'Both a pig and a child eat their food without manners, with no concern for the sensibilities of others, and with the surplus they cannot get into their mouths running down outside in a most disgusting manner. Both a pig and a child make gulping noises when they eat. Both belch loudly, when they should not. The stomachs of both make rumbling sounds at the most inopportune moments.'

'That is true,' said the others. 'These similarities are too plain to be discussed further. We are all familiar with the manners of young children.'

'Both pigs and children cry a great deal, and for no discernible reason,' said one of the Radja's advisers timidly.

'That is true,' said the others. 'That is so true ... They yell, scream, wail, cry, and kick out their legs in a most unpredictable fashion. In some ways, children are even more difficult than women.'

The debate as to the similarities between a child and a young pig went on for a long time, but, when the material was exhausted the people sighed, shrugged their shoulders, and turned once more to the Radja. For their guidance, he said, 'Let us now discuss the *dissimilarities* between a child and a pig. Perhaps we will find so many, that our plan to outwit Rahabaat will have to be given up.'

Brennan-Oan said, 'Well, to start things off, a child can talk and a pig can't.'

The others pondered this, and then said, 'That is a debatable point, at best; but even if true, it is of no importance. Rahabaat means to eat the pig, not to converse with it.'

'Pigs go about naked,' said the High Priest, 'but children, at least those from our better families, wear breech clouts when visitors are expected.'

'There's nothing to prevent our putting a breech clout on a pig,' said the others. 'It's a simple matter to arrange.'

'Pigs go about on four legs,' said the Radja, 'but a child walks on two.' He looked about him, and then added apologetically, 'I don't want to make things more difficult, but that is certainly true.'

'It all depends on the age and temperament of the child,' said the others coldly. 'Many children go about on four legs. This is hardly a difference to be considered seriously.'

The talks went on for a long time, but at last, after every similarity, and every lack of similarity, had been brought into the open and deliberated, the committee came to the conclusion that the one important difference between a pig and a child was the fact that a pig was covered with hair, and a child was not – but that distinction, they said slyly, nudging one another with their elbows, was one that could be easily remedied with a sharp clam shell.

'But a pig, when shaved, is not the beautiful brown of our children,' said Brenan-Oan stubbornly. 'A pig is missionary-colour.'

'Very well! Very well!' said the others angrily. 'We can stain the pig brown . . . There's nothing to prevent our staining the pig with berries, is there?'

So early the next morning, they shaved and stained a young pig. Then they fixed a breech clout about its middle, and, chanting their petition for the return of Mrs Barnfield, they dropped the pig into Rahabaat's crater. A man and a woman who had the most piercing voices on the Island, stood as near the crater as they dared, and when the pig was dropped, they wailed and beat on their breasts.

'Go! Go!' said the man. 'Go, my beautiful son, who is more than life, itself, to me! You might have grown up to support me in my old age, to have made existence sweet for me when I can no longer fish in the ocean for the little I have to live on. But such is not thy destiny. Go, now, to the one I adore more greatly than I do you, thou plump, succulent, adorable son of my loins.'

The woman, pouring gourds full of water into the crater, to simulate the extent of her grief, screamed so loudly that the others of the witnessing party jumped involuntarily, and moved back a little. She said: 'Who am I, who loves Rahabaat so dearly, who has served him, and him alone, since the day of my birth, to deny him now the tasty morsel he desires, even though that morsel be the flesh of my own flesh. Rahabaat's will is my will, and though I shall perpetually mourn the loss of my dear, my only son, whom I can hardly replace at my age of life, the thought of Rahabaat pouting and coveting what is mine can neither be disregarded nor denied.'

Again she screamed, and again she poured water from her dipper.

They continued their ritual of the pig for some months, but with no results at all. They began to wonder if Rahabaat had been as simple as they had hoped, if he were not, instead, deluding them – accepting their gifts willingly enough, but with no sense of reciprocation on his part, since the offerings were, in reality, pigs and not children; and one morning after dropping the pig as usual, they stood around the crater and said in chorus:

'Oh, mighty Rahabaat, whom all adore: we have made sacrifices to you daily of our children, hoping you would grant our wish, and return to us our dear Mrs Barnfield; but although we have faithfully fulfilled our part of the bargain, although we have worshipped you without reservation, and without stinginess, you continue to be stubborn, and set in your divine ways.'

They waited a proper time, and then the High Priest said cautiously, 'If you are not satisfied with our offerings, if you think we've *tricked* you in some way, then show us a sign, so that the remainder of our children may be conserved, may multiply, in

157

time, to do you honour, and to worship your name in another generation.'

Again they paused, and then, as if to show that he had not in the least been taken in by their ruse with the pig, a grumbling sound came from the depths of the crater, followed by a jet of steam, and a short cynical belch of derision; and almost at once three stones, and the pig they had dropped that morning, rose upward in the air and rolled languidly down the side of the volcano.

It was then they knew surely that it was themselves, and not their god, who had been duped; and when they accepted that knowledge at last, they returned to their villages, tearing their hair and weeping, for they knew the only course open to them now. They sat together in miserable groups, their heads bowed, speaking to one another rarely, and then only in whispers. But they had gone too far to turn back now, and that next morning, and each morning thereafter, a child was washed, oiled, per- fumed, and dropped into the volcano, while teams of natives stationed themselves on either side of the cone, and held pointed conversations across the crater.

One team would say in a loud voice: 'It seems to us that when people do a favour for a certain person in high position, that other person, no matter how exalted he happens to be, should, in common fairness, do something in return for the ones we're speaking of now – those loyal, self-sacrificing ones who ask only the favour of Mrs Barnfield's return.'

Then the answer from the other side of the volcano would be: 'That's the way it seems to us, too. It is the way it seems to all who have a remnant of courtesy left in their beings. The laws of politeness, with which we are all familiar, advocate a prompt return of favours, a quick discharge of obligations, as everybody knows; but one, whose name we would not dream of repeating, for fear he might hear us, and hold it against us, seems so old and discourteous that he's lost the common decencies that others observe.'

Then, turning away from the volcano, their sacrifice for that day completed, they would cry out, 'Mrs Barnfield! Mrs Barn- field! Can it be that our happiness no longer concerns you – that you no longer *wish* to return to us? Can it be that you have long since forgotten us?'

In this they did Mrs Barnfield an injustice, for she thought of them almost as often as they thought of her, and planned constantly to come back to them, as she had promised. She had arrived with her husband in Vermont, and had gone with him to the village where his sister lived. His friends advised against their spending a winter alone at the old farm; his sister had asked them to stay in the village with her, at least until Sam had recovered his health.

But Mrs Barnfield was determined that her husband should have his wish, that nobody ruin his last days on earth, and she smiled and said no, to all suggestions. She would manage to make him comfortable on the farm, even though nobody had lived there for years, and the place had gone to ruin. They were accustomed to discomfort; they would get along. It was of no importance that the roads were often impassable in winter: there were snowshoes; there were sleds. If the pump was out of order, she'd have it seen to at once; if it couldn't be fixed, they'd get water from the brook; if the brook froze, what was to stop her from breaking the ice?

So Mrs Barnfield hired a gig, bundled her husband into it, and drove out to his birthplace. Afterwards, he lay all day beside the window, sleeping, or looking out at the road, and, when autumn came, examining the colours of the lovely trees on the hillside. Irma, herself, had little time for contemplation. She was busy from sunrise to sundown, putting the place in order, arranging, planning, providing against the coming winter. Sometimes, Sam's friends, who still remembered him from boyhood, would come to call, and Mrs Barnfield would put him on the front porch, where he could talk and remember the past. Later, it seemed to her that they had been closer during these days that preceded his death than ever before, for no matter how unreasonable he was at times, how great the demands he made upon her, she would pause, close her eyes, and say to herself in pity, 'He's dying. Let him have his way.'

Then cold weather came, and with it the snow he had awaited so long; and as she gave him his breakfast that morning, he said that he had picked out his burial place: it was to be on top of the rocky hill beyond the north field, where he had worked so often as a boy. He took his tea from her, and said. 'Will you see to it that I'm buried there?'

'I'll see to it. You may depend on me.'

'My sister doesn't approve the idea of my being buried out here, so far from town. She wants me buried in her lot in the cemetery, where it will be easier to visit my grave on holidays, and put flowers on it.'

'A man has a right to be buried where he wants to be buried, where that's at all possible. You may put your mind at rest. Your wishes will be respected. You'll be buried on the hill, and no-where else, Mr Barnfield.'

She served him the poached egg and toast she had prepared, and he said queruously that perhaps he was hanging on too long: that before you knew it the ground would freeze so hard that it would be impossible to dig a grave, and that he'd wind up in his sister's lot, after all. The idea obsessed him, and at last Mrs Barnfield said that she'd dig the grave herself, if that would ease his fears. He was afraid she was too frail to perform such a task, and at that Mrs Barnfield laughed, despite herself, and said, 'Me too frail to dig a grave? After all the digging I did on October Island for the past ten years? Why, that's one of the silliest things I ever heard you say!'

That afternoon she wrapped him warmly, and they went to-gether to the place of burial he had selected. She brought out the kitchen rocking chair and seated him in it, so that he could watch, criticize, and see that things were done the way he wanted them. As she worked it began to snow heavily, but he said that he was comfortable, and begged her to finish her task before nightfall; and as she dug among the rocks the pick struck sparks, which sprang outward and were quenched by the snow. She worked for a long time, but at last the grave was deep and wide enough, and she covered it over with boards, and they came into the house to-gether.

He died in January, when it was below zero, and the following day they buried him on the rocky hill, the way he wanted it. Those in the village who still remembered him stood there quietly in the cold, steam coming from their mouths and nostrils as they moved about and stamped their feet on the frozen earth; but during the long prayer it began to snow once more, and before the men could fill the grave with earth, it had filled up first with snow.

When it was over, when the last spadeful of earth had fallen on his coffin, Mrs Barnfield wept, despite her resolution, not for the happiness she had lost, but for the happiness he might have given but had denied her. The neighbours who came with her into the house gathered about her and said, 'Here now! None of that! These things happen, and we must bear them somehow.'

Afterwards, she missed him as one misses an old piece of furniture which for years has filled a familiar place in a house; but she missed him without sorrow and without regret, and immediately she began planning a future without him. During these first days of her widowhood she thought constantly of the Island she had lost, and often at night when she could not sleep, she would go to her window, turn her face in the direction of October Island, and whisper in a small, wheedling voice, 'Pray for me! Please continue to pray for my return. Really, you're not praying half hard enough. This is a difficult situation that's going to require the earnest efforts of us all.'

As though obeying her, the people of October Island continued their prayers, their hints, and their sacrifices for some months to come, their voices getting more strained, their faces more tense; but do what they would, Rahabaat was impervious to their prayers. They went about in an atmosphere of depression, avoiding one another's eyes, muttering to themselves of Rahabaat's indifference, as their hopes diminished. Each morning, as before, they selected a child and dropped it into the crater, and the wails of the people, and the dialogue of those whose duty it was to upbraid their god in chorus and remind him of his obligation, rang out through the morning.

They said, 'Oh, senile and blind Rahabaat: we ask so little in return for the courtesies we grant you. We ask only that Mrs Barnfield come to us again, this time alone, and that our Golden Age commence at once as has been prophesied.'

Chapter Fifteen

WHEN Captain Hansen called at October Island on his summer trip that year he found the inhabitants in a state of depression. There was nobody at the mole to greet him and this time nobody came to trade. The few people he saw went about slowly, their eyes lowered, their shoulders sagging, as though in mourning, and when he tried to question them, they looked at him oddly and shook their heads, as though determined to tell him nothing. Later, the Radja and Brenan-Oan came aboard to ask if he had heard from Mrs Barnfield; when he said he had not, they glanced despairingly at each other and, without speaking again, turned away.

He did not stay in port long, only long enough to replenish his fresh water; by late afternoon he was at sea again. He thought of Mrs Barnfield on his return to Hawaii, wondering what had become of her, why she had not written him as he had expected. He came to the conclusion that, despite her optimism, neither he nor the other October Islanders would ever see her again; but in this he was mistaken, for when his schooner arrived at her regular berth in Honolulu, this remarkable woman was sitting on a pineapple crate at shipside, ready to rush forward and greet him.

He came down the gang-plank at once, and she shook his hand warmly. He stared at her, for in her new clothes she looked more like a duchess on her way to a garden party than a missionary pledged to the saving of primitive souls. She laughed nervously, and said, 'I know the first question on your tongue. I'll answer it before it's asked: I'm a widow: Mr Barnfield died in January.' She shook out her skirts and continued, 'I should be wearing mourning, but, as you see, I'm not.' She raised her lavender silk-and-lace sunshade. 'I have so much to tell you, I hardly know where to begin,' she said.

He still had not spoken, and she went on: 'I know this is a bad time to talk to you, but there was something I had to tell you before you saw the agents, and discovered it through them. So I found out when you were due in port, and I've been on the look-out for you, and here I am.' Then, glancing about her, she added, 'Please go about your duties. I won't be in your way at all. But don't question me right now. Later on, I'll tell you everything, although some of it is strange and you'll find it hard to believe.'

Captain Hansen shouted an order over his shoulder, and then, turning back to Mrs Barnfield, he laughed and said, 'I'll believe it. Don't worry about that.'

'The main thing I had to tell you,' said Mrs Barnfield, 'is that the *Mattie B. Powell* is now your property, the way you wanted it.' Then, seeing his mouth opening in disbelief, she added quickly, 'You need have no fear of the proprieties being violated. The schooner is less a gift from me, than a gift from God, and as such you can hardly object to what I've done as agent for you both.'

'I see,' he said doubtfully.

'My return is a miracle worked by the Lord,' said Mrs Barnfield. 'You see, I prayed diligently that I could somehow return, and at last my prayers were answered – through the medium of a person I once knew, a person I'd not heard from in years, and from whom I had no right to expect anything at all: in short, I'm referring to my sister Lurline, of whom you've often heard me speak.'

They stepped back from the pier to let a group of stevedores pass, and Mrs Barnfield continued: 'It happened most opportunely for me, I must say. It was last March and I had almost nothing to live on – only this little pension from the church – and since I had no relatives, being the last one on both sides of the family, it looked as though I'd have to spend the rest of my life with Mr Barnfield's sister, as much as I disliked that prospect. I didn't want to be a burden, so I took in sewing, and that helped out a little; but every night I prayed to be returned to October Island, and those I love there, and God heard my prayers eventually, and granted them just when I'd almost lost faith in His goodness and loving-kindness.'

Captain Hansen nodded in sympathy, but did not speak.

'Lurline died in Mobile without making a will, and so I got this letter about her death. I went to Mobile at once to present credentials of my kinship, as they instructed me to. Well, the upshot of the matter was that I was declared her sole heir. I was surprised, I must confess, when I learned the estate was substantially more than a hundred thousand dollars. So I got the money and here I am talking to you in Hawaii, on my way back to October Island. It couldn't have worked out better.'

She paused significantly, and added: 'At the finish of my prayers, I invariably appended a prayer on your behalf – a prayer that you be given the *Mattie B. Powell*, since you once told me that was your dearest wish; so, since both prayers were linked together, I concluded naturally enough, for it's the only logical conclusion, that both had been answered, and I arranged to have my inheritance transferred to a bank here in Honolulu. This was done last week, about the same time that I arrived.'

He stared at her as though a little stunned, his eyes on guard, as if waiting for her to laugh at his credulity and tell him it was all a joke she'd made up for his amusement.

She said, 'I bought the schooner for you last Wednesday, and the transaction is now complete, with the vessel registered in your name. We'll go together tomorrow and see the lawyers. They'll explain things to you much better than I can. I paid fifteen thousand five hundred dollars for her, which isn't too bad, I understand.'

He shook his head from side to side and said in a weak voice, 'I see!'

She'd taken a room at Mrs Cuthbert's boarding-house, she continued, and suggested that he come that night to dinner, where they could discuss things in greater detail. There was a private parlour, which she'd also engaged, and they'd be alone and undisturbed.

He started to speak, but she raised her hand and said, 'Later! Everything in time! I'll tell you everything you want to know, but you mustn't rush me.' Then, turning suddenly, she signalled her cab with her sunshade, shook hands again, lifted her skirts to her ankles, and hurried down the long wharf.

When they were alone in Mrs Cuthbert's private parlour, with its doyleys, its canaries, its flowers under glass and gilded reeds in red lacquer vases, Mrs Barnfield spoke in detail of Sam's last day. Then, shifting to her sister and her inheritance, she asked, 'Do you remember, years ago, mailing a letter I'd written Lurline – a letter asking her to live with Mr Barnfield and me if she had no other place to go?'

Captain Hansen remembered the letter perfectly, and she gave him the facts she'd learned since about her sister. The letter had been of vital importance, for, if she had never written it, Lurline's fortune, in all probability, would have gone to the State of

Alabama, and not to herself. But she must apologize for telling these things in such a haphazard way! She must organize her thoughts, eliminating all irrelevant matters, and even deleting many of the interesting but unrelated things she'd discovered about her sister's life!

It was warm in the parlour, and they decided, when their dinner was finished, to walk together along the beach. They did so, her hand resting lightly on his forearm as though she, of all people, needed support. She guided him to a bench fronting the sea and they sat there with the breeze on their faces. When she was settled she drew her brows together in thought, nodded twice, and said that after Lurline bought the house in Mobile, she had nailed up the windows and all the doors, except one.

'Lurline became a sort of public character,' she continued. 'At first she went out in the day to buy food or the other things she needed. She'd walk down the street in her strange clothes, attracting the attention of everybody with her stare and her peculiar habits. She was like an island, and people told me that no matter how crowded the street was, she never touched anybody. She'd turn like a dancer, pivot, balance on her toes, pause a second, and then go on her way, walking very fast, without so much as brushing against a sleeve.'

Captain Hansen picked up a palmful of sand and allowed it to trickle through his fingers, nodding his head from time to time.

'I spent several weeks in Mobile, while matters were being straightened out,' said Irma, 'and I talked to people and found out a lot of things about Lurline, and what her life had been. Nobody knew her name, but everybody called her "Miss Garpiddy", of all things.'

'It's a peculiar name,' said Captain Hansen. 'What does it mean?'

'I'll come to that later,' said Irma; 'but let me go on in my own way ... As I said before, Lurline would come out in the daytime, at first, and sometimes she'd even talk to people; but later on she'd come out only at twilight, and wander about the city like a ghost.'

'I've been in Mobile,' said Captain Hansen. 'I used to know it well.'

Mrs Barnfield nodded, and said, 'For a while, Lurline had

165

water and gas, and paid her bills, too; but as her stinginess grew on her like a disease, she gave them up as things she couldn't afford. She quit buying food, too. They said she never begged, and that she wouldn't accept things from people. Towards the end of her life she lived on what she could find in garbage pails.'

Mrs Barnfield covered her face with her hands. 'Oh, it's shameful!' she said. 'The whole thing is shameful!'

When she recovered herself, she went on: 'It wasn't that Lurline was a miser, as people said. I don't think that was the reason at all. I think she was afraid of money, the way some people are afraid of cats, or locked rooms, or caterpillars. She was afraid of it – and, of course, she loved it dearly, too!'

From the first, continued Mrs Barnfield, Lurline had been the true collector, for everything abandoned by others had, through the very fact of its abandonment, taken on value for her. She brought home old newspapers, tin cans, jugs, bottles, driftwood, discarded shoes – anything that she could save, preserve, stack, and keep; and when she'd discovered this fact about her sister, she'd known how Lurline must have spent her days in that dark, dismal house: she'd spent them sorting, counting, cataloguing in her mind, arranging, and rearranging, her possessions in piles and bundles and heaps.

She had started her collection in the bedroom, piling the material as high as the ceiling, building little concealed caves, and leaving narrow, intricate alleyways through which she could sidle, or, perhaps, hide if attacked by the vague terrors, which, she felt, were outside to destroy her.

'Was she crazy?' asked Captain Hansen in a soft voice.

'I don't know,' said Irma. 'Frankly, I don't know, although I've thought about it often enough. I talked to everybody who'd known her, but I didn't find out much until I went to the neighbourhood where she'd lived. There were mostly coloured people in that part of town, and they told me things they wouldn't tell anybody else, because I was her sister, and they felt I had the right to know, as it might comfort me. That's how I found out the origin of her nickname. The Negroes had given it to her, and called her that; but others had misunderstood what they said and had corrupted the name, as you'll soon see.'

She lowered her head, and then stopped speaking as a couple approached down the walk. After they had passed, she went on:

'The Negroes understood her and pitied her, being outcasts, too, in a way. Sometimes, when they hadn't seen her for a few days but knew she was inside her house, they'd stand outside her window in the dark. They'd scratch on the blinds, and whisper, "Miss God Pity! Miss God Pity! Are you feeling well?" And then Lurline would find her way through those lanes of dirt and junk, and put her lips to the blinds, and say in her soft, hoarse voice, "God pity you, too. God pity us all." '

'Later, when they really trusted me, the Negroes told me they knew the night she died. She'd been very weak, and she'd been alone in that dark place for days. They gathered about her window, and standing there they could hear her breathing heavily, and crying to herself. They scratched on the blinds and called to her, asking if there was anything she wanted; but this time Lurline wouldn't answer, or maybe she couldn't answer, and at last the sounds stopped, and they knew she was dead.'

Mrs Barnfield paused, and then said, 'When the police came later and forced an entry into the house, they found Lurline on a pallet of old rags and sacks.' She waited again, her face turned away from the sea. When she had recovered herself, she said quietly, 'She died of starvation, with all the money within arm's reach.'

The police had tried to establish her identity, but all they learned was what the real estate people, from whom she'd bought the house, could tell them. She might have been buried as the Widow Bessie Pigg, and her true identity never known; but one of the policemen spotted the telescope-bag, and pulled it out from the bottom of its particular pile of junk. As he did so the straps broke, and twenty-dollar bills spilled out and rustled over his shoes. After that they went through everything carefully: they found money tucked away everywhere.

'And then, when all that junk had been sifted and examined piece by piece,' said Mrs Barnfield, 'they found the letter I'd written back in 1895. She'd never opened it, but the police opened it quickly enough, and when they'd read it through they knew her name was Lurline Huffstetter, and that she had a sister Irma, who was married to a Huhnerite missionary named Barnfield, and lived with him on October Island. After that, it was easy. You know the rest.'

Mrs Barnfield got up, and Captain Hansen followed her. They walked leisurely towards Mrs Cuthbert's place, and Irma said, 'Everybody wondered about the letter, and everybody had an explanation of his own.' She laughed gently, and added, 'I wonder what your explanation is?'

Captain Hansen said that several explanations had come to mind while Mrs Barnfield was telling her story. The one he liked best was this: Lurline had been as surprised when she got the letter in Philadelphia as the police had been when they found it in Mobile. She hadn't heard from her sister in many years; she'd almost come to the conclusion that Irma no longer existed; the letter brought back her past sharply to her. She was afraid to open the letter, as though it might stir up all sorts of memories that were better left as they were.

Mrs Barnfield thought that a reasonable explanation, and Captain Hansen continued: 'But I think she meant to read the letter sooner or later, and that's why she brought it with her, even though she left practically everything else behind. But she waited too long, and the trap caught her. I think she tossed the letter into a cupboard finally, and it became the cornerstone of her collection of bottles and cans and old pieces of wood. Afterwards, she never thought of it as anything but that.'

Mrs Barnfield laughed again, and shook her head in mild dissent; Captain Hansen asked, 'What do you think happened? What's your own solution?'

'Oh, it's much simpler than yours,' she said. 'I think Lurline acted the way she did because she's peculiar. That's all there is to it, in my opinion.'

She added that her sister was a complete enigma to her. She had made every effort to understand the processes of her mind, but having failed, she was determined, now, to enjoy the money she'd so unexpectedly received, and to dismiss the giver from her mind as one who defied understanding.

They reached the boarding-house, and Irma stopped at the gate and said, 'There's a request I want to make of you, but there's no reason for your granting it, unless you really want to do so ... Now, here's what I'd like for you to do! I'd like for you to change the name of the schooner from the *Mattie B. Powell* to the *Irma H. Barnfield*.'

'That'll be easy enough to handle,' he said.

'It isn't all vanity on my part,' she said, 'although there's vanity in it.'

'We'll make the change tomorrow.'

Mrs Barnfield said, an apologetic softness in her voice, that if he considered her a silly old woman whose sentimentality carried her beyond the boundaries of good taste, she could not blame him, for that, perhaps, was precisely what she was. Nevertheless, it would be pleasant, particularly in the night, when she was alone on October Island and could not sleep, to visualize his dear face and figure, and to think of him treading her decks.

Chapter Sixteen

At last everything was in order, and the *Irma H. Barnfield*, with her passenger aboard, sailed for October Island. She had long talks with Captain Hansen. She told him all her thoughts. She discussed her mother and father, and, most of all, the perverse career of her sister Lurline. It was a strange thing, she felt, but it almost seemed to her that the *good* people she'd known, who'd loved her, had done little for her; but Lurline, who'd hated her so openly, had made her dreams come true with her *badness*. It was a most puzzling situation, a thing she wanted to turn over and over in her mind until she understood its implications a little better.

One night after they had finished dinner, and still sat together at table, she said, 'I know of course that you aren't a *married* man, but perhaps I'm not nearly so innocent as some people think. Now, tell me one thing frankly: did you ever indulge in a love affair?' He hesitated, and she added, 'I'm not referring to an affair of the spirit, or anything of that sort. I'm not referring to friendship, or admiration, or respect. I mean just what you think I mean: have you ever known carnal love?'

'Why, yes. Since you bring the matter up, I have.'

'Seldom, or often.'

'Often, Mrs Barnfield.'

'How often, Captain Hansen?'

He took up his fork and traced a pattern on the cloth with it. He was plainly embarrassed, but he looked steadily into her eyes and said, 'As often as I've been able to arrange it, Mrs Barnfield.'

'You always impressed me as a warm, sensual man,' she said, 'but of course I wanted to be sure.' She took a sip of water from her glass, and then went on, 'Now that we've established your temperament, I want to ask my second question: Is carnal love all that it's supposed to be?'

His neck turned red, and he moved his fork back and forth across the cloth. After a moment he said, 'Why are you so interested?' But he kept thinking to himself, 'My God! Is this to be the price of my schooner?'

'You hear so much about the joys of love that it makes you stop and wonder at times,' she said. 'There are all those romantic figures that novelists and poets write about – people who die for love, renounce the world for love, or do any number of peculiar things for it. Now, if it's really that remarkable, it seems a shame to miss it ... But you haven't answered my question, so I'll ask it again : 'Is carnal love all it's cracked up to be?'

Captain Hansen made a little pyramid of spoons and forks on the table, then, speaking cautiously, he said, 'Opinions vary in these matters, but as far as I'm concerned, I consider it all it's cracked up to be.'

'Thank you for your honesty,' she said. 'It's a comfort to have a true friend like yourself ... Now, the real point of my inquiry is this : while Mr Barnfield was alive, I was bound to him by my vows at the altar, and of course I couldn't even contemplate such things; but since he's passed on I feel free to live my life as I choose to live it.'

'Are you figuring on a love affair of your own?' asked Captain Hansen after a short silence.

'Well, it isn't quite that definite,' she said. 'But the High Priest intimated on several occasions that when I returned alone the people would be pleased if I took a consort, since the terms of the prophecy would be fulfilled by that time, and it wouldn't matter what I did. Of course, I can have my pick of the Island.'

'Do you have anybody particularly in mind?'

'Frankly, no, Captain Hansen, although I suppose any of the young men of the Island – and there are several most attractive ones, I must say – would do. But I'm in a quandary, as the whole thing seems a bother at my time of life. After all, I'm fifty-three, as you know. That's why I was so anxious to get the frank opinion of a man of experience, like yourself – a man whose opinion I can trust.'

He thought a moment, and then said, 'Since things have worked out so well for you this far, I'd advise you to continue the way you are. That seems to be the most sensible way of handling the matter.'

She pressed his hand with relief and thanked him for his advice, which, she confessed, coincided with her own wishes: then, feeling that she had made him uncomfortable with her frankness, she changed the subject abruptly, and talked of

October Island: the things she hoped to accomplish there; how fond she was of the people, and how she looked forward to being among them once more.

On October Island itself the natives had long since abandoned the tactful approach to Rahabaat, and now they shouted insults at him.

'It is not alone for ourselves that we ask the return of Mrs Barnfield,' they said. 'It is for your glory, too. The prophecy said she would come when your name was repudiated everywhere, when others laughed at your pretensions. Then send her to us now, for this is the moment, for even ourselves, the ones that remained faithful to you, now laugh you to scorn.'

'Yes,' said the answering group. 'Only we, a poor handful, have remained faithful, or remembered your past glories. But we, too, will repudiate you, as others have done, unless this simple favour is granted, and granted quickly.

'And when we have repudiated you, when we no longer remember what others have long since forgotten, your name will pass out of the minds of men, and you will be dead, indeed.'

Then all together the people wailed and cried out, 'Tricky Rahabaat! Unscrupulous Rahabaat! Selfish Rahabaat who takes, but does not give in return! Our politeness is played out. Give us our prayer or we will curse you! We will tell strangers of your laziness and impotence! We will blacken you with shame!'

But all their prayers, all their criticism, all their despair, seemed neither to rouse Rahabaat, nor spur him to action, and at last there were few children left on the Island to offer him. Then, some days later, when hope was almost gone, one of the young men looked towards the horizon at the moment the sun freed itself from the sea and lifted above it. He shouted, turned to his fellows, and pointed excitedly, for there coming towards them was a schooner under full sail. It was plainly the *Mattie B. Powell* returning out of season. This was a point of most encouraging significance, but their sufferings had taught them caution, and they waited doubtfully as the schooner, under the power of the morning breeze, tacked and approached the lagoon. They strained their eyes towards her, seeking the sign they prayed for, but did not dare expect to see; and then one of the men shouted out, 'She is there! She is returning to us!' He ran about in circles saying, 'There! There standing at the rail. You can see

172

her plainly now. It is a woman beyond doubt. It is our friend returning to us.'

In a short time the figure was plain to all, and at the sight of Mrs Barnfield, the people embraced one another and wept with a sort of nervous joy; then, when their first emotions of jubilation were expended, they hurried down the sides of the volcano, some of them going to the home of their patron to clean it, and to decorate it with flowers and fruits, others racing to the harbour to stand there and chatter together,

The schooner was coming closer now, was approaching the reef beyond the lagoon, and the lookout, who had never left his post, cried out, 'Look! There's a man standing at the bow of the boat. Now, he is approaching Mrs Barnfield. Now, they are talking together.'

It was Captain Hansen himself. He had called his passenger a little before sunrise, as she had asked him to, and she had joined him promptly on deck. He passed his binoculars to her, and when she saw the excitement of the natives, and visualized the welcome that waited her, she went to her cabin to put on her priestly robes for them. Now, Captain Hansen lifted his glasses again, and watched the Islanders as they ran hysterically up and down the narrow beach. Listening, he could hear their voices as they shouted, and even the sound of their distant flutes and finger-drums; and he lowered his glasses and sighed at the warmth of this welcome, which was not for himself.

Mrs Barnfield, dressed in her flowing white robes, joined him a moment later, and he handed her the binoculars. The sounds from the Island were clearer now, more definable in their purpose, and Irma, watching the natives, said quickly, 'But how did they know I was coming back at all?'

She thought of her first landing, and regretted that Mr Barnfield was not present to share her triumph. She lowered her head and sighed, then, recovering herself, she turned resolutely, knowing this was no time for grief, but a time for joy. The schooner was nearing the entrance to the lagoon, and the welcome from the beach was increasing in its intensity. She pressed forward against the rail, waved her hand, and blew a kiss to her worshippers. At once they began to scream louder, and to dance about the beach.

Some of them plunged into the water, and swam towards the

vessel. When they reached it, they frolicked like welcoming porpoises, diving, turning, and coming to the surface to laugh and shake water from their hair, their teeth shining in the morning sunlight; but at last, when the schooner was abreast of the mole, and the people had moored it there securely, Irma came to the rail once more, while the natives, in an ecstasy of exhilaration, capered, cried out, and pelted her with flowers.

In her own excitement, she laughed too; then, collecting her thoughts, she held up her hand for silence and began her official speech of return. She explained that she had not once been happy after she had left October Island, for it appeared that the land she had always thought of as being her home, was not, in reality, her true home at all. October Island was her true home, she said, and not the silly, terrifying world that lay outside it; and now that her husband was dead, she had returned as quickly as she could to those she loved, and who loved her in return. She was deeply moved by the welcome she had received, and she promised never to leave the Island again.

When she had finished the Islanders began one of the hymns she had taught them, accompanying themselves with their pebble-gourds, their drums, and their marimbas. Mrs Barnfield tilted her head and listened critically to this hymn of welcome. There was surely something wrong with the hymn, she thought, although she could not say precisely what it was. The words seemed accurate enough, and the tune itself was reasonably true; but there was an excitement about it, a certain sensuousness that should not be there, that no hymns should have, and she shook her head in disapproval, and listened.

When it was finished she looked about her, and then she knew the thing that had bothered her unconsciously from the moment of her arrival. She said in surprise, 'But where are the children? What has become of all the children?'

She beckoned to Captain Hansen, and when he stood beside her in the secondary place on honour, she finished her speech. She told of her unexpected inheritance, and how it had made her return possible. They did not understand what she was talking about, but they listened intently; and when she had finished she shook hands with Captain Hansen, and descended the companionway briskly. At once the natives lifted her in their arms, so that no dirt should touch her sacred foot, and carried her to a flower-decked throne that they had prepared in anticipation of her return. They seated her on it, took the pins from her hair, and allowed it to fall loosely about her.

She laughed indulgently, striking at them with her fan, saying, 'You musntn't! Really, you mustn't! ... My hair isn't *that* pretty!'

They put a head-dress of feathers about her forehead and anointed her brows, lips, and hands with an ointment of particular fragrance. The High Priest gave her the cup and spoon to hold in her right hand, and Brenau-Oan gave her Kaplinja's thigh-bone for her left; and raising these emblems of her power, she smiled and looked languidly about her.

When the ceremony which had turned Mrs Barnfield into a deity was over, the natives lifted the throne to their shoulders, and riding there high above her subjects, Mrs Barnfield laughed easily, fluffed out her hair, and called out impatiently, 'But where are the children? Really, you must tell me where the *children* are!'

Suddenly Captain Hansen was sick of this kind, opinionated, generous, stupid, courageous old woman, and as she disappeared with her worshippers around a curve in the beach, he knew that he never wanted to see her again, that he was through with her for ever. In a short time he must commence unloading the supplies Mrs Barnfield had brought with her, all the presents she had selected in Honolulu for her friends on the Island; but for the time being, before the sun was too high in the sky, he wanted to stand here and consider Mrs Barnfield and her works.

Once, a long time ago, when he had first left October Island, and his ship was in dry dock in San Francisco, he had passed a theatre at which a musical piece was playing. He had never been to the theatre, and hoping the experience would give him a better understanding of the lives and customs of Americans, he bought a ticket and went inside.

Even after all these years he still remembered that wonderful evening, for the principals had been in good voice, the music tuneful, the costumes new and elaborate, and the girls beautiful. As the evening advanced, the plot of the piece became more and more involved, until, at length, there seemed no way out at all; but sitting alone in the darkened theatre, in a strange land he had not seen before that morning, he accepted the play as real

175

in every detail, until, at length, a stranger appeared in the final scene to set matters right for everyone: to clear the overseer of the forgery charge; to pay off the mortgage on the pineapple farm; to end the misunderstanding that kept the secondary lovers apart; to reveal that the handsome but penniless tenor was actually a prince, and, as such, worthy to marry an American girl.

It was at this point that he doubted the play's validity, and he had shaken his head in disbelief, saying, 'Things don't happen that way. It's not true to life.' But now, remembering what Mrs Barnfield had accomplished for others, he wondered if his judgement had not been a little hasty. Certainly it was true that, through her efforts, he now owned a splendid schooner; that Sam Barnfield had his cold grave on a bleak hill, precisely as he desired it; that the Islanders had their goddess and her cup filled with milk; that Irma, herself, had the inexhaustible adoration she craved . . .

When he said the play was untrue to life, did he not really mean it was untrue to his experience, to the special logic that gave his own life consequence, and made it tolerable? He moved his hands slowly along the rail, thinking that if we desire greatly enough, if we seek with a proper diligence, all strange things – even happiness, the strangest of all – become true to life at the end. Perhaps that was the meaning the divided ones like himself, who have peace nowhere in the world, seek with such desperation, and rarely find.